PRAISE FOR JACQUIE BIGGAR

The Player by Jacquie Biggar

I've read work by Jacquie Biggar before and I love her writing style, I am easily transported in to her story and the lives of her characters. This story definitely had me laughing my way through it! The banter between Roy and Patience certainly kept me entertained from beginning to end; they definitely knew how to rub each other up the wrong way!!

— KATIE MATTHEWS

The Player by Jacquie Biggar is another one of my favorites. As a professional hockey player Roy was used to having his pick of women, but then one of those women turns into a stalker. Now he needs help cleaning up his image. Will he settle down and forget his bachelor ways? This story had me on the edge of my seat wanting to know what was going to happen.

— BOOKBUB REVIEW

Jacquie Biggar's story the Player that took the cherry! I love sports stories (especially hockey ones) and Jacquie gives us Roy who gets sidelined from NHL thanks to his stalker ex so he ends up needing some little help from a PA Patience ... so you can imagine the good laughs and antics and aww moments she mixed up for us and to be frank, I think the story would have deserved to be longer! I for sure will keep my eyes open for more by Jacquie!

— JANA T.

SUNSET BEACH

SUNSET BEACH

BLUE HAVEN- BOOK 2

JACQUIE BIGGAR

WAVEFRONT PUBLISHING

This is a work of fiction. Characters, names, places, and incidents are either the product of the author's imagination or are used fictitiously, and any resemblance to actual persons, living or dead, business establishments, locales, or events is entirely coincidental.

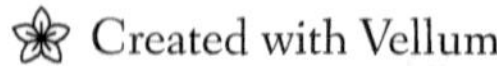

This one is for my critique partners, you know who you are.

Without your patience and guidance when I get carried away, these stories could not shine.

I am incredibly grateful for all that you've done for me throughout the years.

Jacquie

If you are not too long, I will wait here for you all my life.

— OSCAR WILDE

INTRODUCTION

An explosive secret threatens the peace and tranquility of Sweetheart Cove

Single father Trace Michaels has his hands full coping with a rebellious teenage daughter, troublesome ex-wife, and campaigning for the mayor's election. He doesn't have time to get distracted by an old flame from his past-- one he's never forgotten.

When an unknown source leaks surprising news that could damage his career, Trace turns to the one person he trusts for the truth.

Single mother Mona Samuels knows how difficult it can be to raise a daughter. She empathizes with

Trace, but when he comes to her for advice, she's conflicted. They say the truth will set you free but unburying the past could destroy everything she's worked so hard to build.

PREFACE

Mona sighed her relief when the Betsy Boop showed up on the horizon. Troy was about as reliable as they came, but she'd still been worried about her cargo. The diner was low on a number of items, thanks to the recent storms. That was the problem with living on an island, you had to count on the weather in order to survive. The ferries had canceled most of their runs for the week due to rough seas. She'd been lucky to get this short pocket in the weather systems so Troy could do a run for her. Funny thing about bad weather; it was great for business.

The plane circled above Sweetheart Cove a couple of times before coming in for a smooth splashdown on the moody blue-gray water. As she bundled up for her walk down the dock, the door opened, and the grizzled pilot stepped out to secure the moorings. Mona raised her hand in a wave, but Troy had already turned back to the plane and lifted out a dark blue suitcase ahead of another man's descent.

Curious, Mona slowed her pace, allowing the new arrival to get his bearings on semi-solid ground. That is, until she realized *who* had just arrived with her produce—Trace Michaels.

Dammit, it was too late to beat a hasty retreat. She was going to have to buck up and act the responsible businesswoman she'd become, instead of the rebellious teenager who'd had her heart broken thanks to this man.

Troy noticed her first. "Made good time, today. Were you waiting long?"

She smiled at the pilot; aware Trace had stiffened at her appearance. "Not more than five minutes. I owe you a big piece of pie for this, Troy. You saved me from a whole lot of unhappy customers."

"Oh, I can't believe that." Troy grinned, good-naturedly. "Sweet Treats is packed anytime I come to town. I'll need to start phoning for a reservation, soon."

Mona laughed. "You come around back to the kitchen and I'll find you a seat. We'd be lost without you," she added, and was pleased to see him blush.

He glanced from her to Trace, seeming to pick up on the icy undercurrents. "Well, I'd best get this stock unloaded so you can go about your day." He shook

Trace's hand. "Thanks again, Mr. Michaels. I'll tell my Betsy to give you a call."

"You do that." Trace clapped the man on the back and picked up his suitcase to stride toward Mona. "Hi," he said quietly, coming to a stop way too close for comfort.

Even as she took a step back, needing to maintain a physical as well as mental distance between them, she couldn't help falling into those eyes. They said the eyes were the window to a person's soul and she'd always believed it until Trace betrayed her and yet denied it the entire time. His electric blue eyes, so startling with dark hair, had convinced her he was telling the truth when it had been nothing but lies. But hey, that was seventeen, almost eighteen, years ago—she'd gotten over him.

Yeah, right.

"Spending the taxpayer's dime on private vacations, Trace? I'm sure it will go over big with your constituency." Not that they would care, he had half the town in love with him. And how did he manage to get better looking the more he aged, while she... didn't?

"Still packing that chip on your shoulder, I see," he murmured with a slight smile. "Actually, I was on a business trip sanctioned by the board—sorry to disappoint." He glanced over his shoulder as Troy unloaded the first of the heavy crates. "Do you need a hand getting your stock to a vehicle? I assume you brought something larger than that toy car you like to drive?"

He knew what she drove? Well, of course he did. It wasn't like they lived in a huge metropolis. Sweetheart Cove boasted a healthy population of seven thousand which swelled to double the size in the tourist season—or at least, it had.

"I borrowed Jacob's truck, and no thanks. I have someone coming to help me. As a matter of fact, there he is now." She heaved a silent sigh of gratitude as Jason pulled up on his motorbike, the engine giving a throaty growl before he shut it down.

"New boyfriend?" Trace asked, his smile fading.

"New... something," Mona agreed with a brief flare of satisfaction. He may have moved on from their relationship, but there were still dark waters under the bridge. "Samantha mentioned Beth was spending the night; are you good with that?" She may harbor complicated emotions for her father, but Beth was a joy to be around. Someday she would have to sit the girls down and have a serious conversation with them. She just hoped they wouldn't hate her after the truth came out.

"Of course, though I think they're planning on the weekend. I'll call Beth in the morning and tell her to come home." Trace glanced at the expensive-looking watch on his wrist. "If you're good here, I better take off. I still have a few hours of paperwork ahead of me."

He rubbed the back of his neck, exhaustion darkening his eyes. "Take care of yourself, Mona."

She took a deep breath, inhaling the masculine, citrus and pine scent of his body as he brushed by her on the narrow dock. In all the years they'd been apart, her heart still recognized him. It was both thrilling and painful.

She crossed her arms as Jason joined her after a barely-there nod from Trace before he disappeared over the rise. "Thanks for coming."

"No problem," he said, his gaze sharpening on her face. "Was that guy giving you grief? I could—"

Mona shook her head and dropped her arms. "No, it's fine. He's the father of one of my daughter's friends—we were just talking." She steered the conversation away from personal matters. "So, you ready to haul my groceries?"

"Yes, ma'am." He grinned. "That's why you pay me the big bucks."

"Huh, was getting paid part of our agreement? I thought you were my apprentice." She laughed at his expression. "I'm kidding. Okay, let's get this stuff out of the sun, it cost me an arm and a leg."

She couldn't resist one last forbidden look at the shoreline, hoping to catch sight of Trace—but he was gone.

SUNSET BEACH

BLUE HAVEN #2

1

Mayor Trace Michaels glanced out of the floatplane's narrow window at the ribbon of rocky, evergreen-covered islands threading through the Pacific Ocean. Still a way to go before they reached Blue Haven Island. He frowned over the reports on his laptop. The new tax base he'd lobbied the board for was hurting Sweetheart Cove financially. The local economy counted on a combination of the logging industry and tourism, both of which were suffering under the current provincial government's agendas. He needed a new plan of action, and soon, or he'd be marketing his hometown as a ghost town.

Troy glanced over his shoulder from the pilot's seat. "Was this a business or pleasure trip, Mr. Michaels? You don't get away from the island all that often, do you?"

Why leave when everyone he cared about was on Blue Haven? He avoided answering the well-meaning pilot's question with one of his own. "How's that lovely daughter of yours, Troy? Betsy still away at college?"

The other man nodded and tapped his dash. "Yes, sir. This old girl, Betsy Boop, is paying her way through a business major. Maybe she could get a job with the town when she's done?" He cleared his throat. "Be great if she didn't get it in her head to leave the island for good, you know?"

Yeah, Trace understood exactly where he was coming from. His own daughter was making noises about traveling abroad, and it worried him sick.

"Tell her to get in touch with me when she finishes her courses and we'll figure something out," he told Troy. "We single fathers need to stick together." He smiled and lowered his head, focusing on the depressing numbers in the spreadsheet. They needed something to hook tourists and bring them flocking to the island, but what?

His ex-wife had opened a new health spa on a stretch of prime beach property amid demonstrations from the townspeople. He hadn't agreed with her methods, but the concept was a good one—they just needed to build on the idea. Environmentally conscious, exclusive vacations—could that be the answer?

"There she is, Mr. Michaels, home sweet home." Troy banked left and flew over the lower tip of Blue Haven's heart-shaped coastline. The town came next, huddled in the bosom of rolling hills that protected the small community from the worst of nature's wrath. The plane nosed downward, angling for the long wooden dock jutting into the harbor.

His cell phone jingled a tune to Beth's favorite boy band, The Jonas Brothers. He grimaced and jabbed the button, ending the noise. "I thought I asked you *not* to play with my ringer." He'd born the teasing because of his daughter's music choices all too often in the past, but at least they'd had the same taste in music. Now though... not so much.

"Is that how you always answer the phone? I thought I taught *you* better manners," his smart-alecky daughter answered.

Touché.

Trace closed his laptop and sighed. Why did they always butt heads? "Let's try this again; hello, Bethany, to what do I owe this call?"

"Da... ad." She sighed right back. "You know I hate when you call me that." She didn't wait for his reply, no doubt because she'd heard it a thousand times. "Can I spend the night at Samantha's? We want to go over details for my birthday party—sixteen is kind of a big deal. I want it to be perfect."

Sixteen. Where had his baby girl gone? A collage of bittersweet memories played out in his head. Sally never wanted responsibility for a child and had turned Beth's custody over without a fuss. It was one of the only times he could remember having a moment's affection for his wife.

"Dad, did you hear me?" Beth said with all the impatience of a teenager.

"Sorry, I was remembering when you were a cute, *respectful* child," he muttered. "Yes, you can stay with Samantha—as long as you cleared it with her mother first. No more surprise visits, got it?" Mona had reamed him out the last time the two girls pulled that prank, blaming him for not being there for his kid.

"Great," Beth chortled, all happified now she was getting her way. "Wait until you see what we have planned—it's going to be epic! Okay, Dad, see you Sunday. Bye." And click, she was gone.

Sunday? Who said anything about Sunday? Last time he checked, spending the night meant one day, as in twenty-four hours, not a mini vacation. Trace started to dial her back, then closed down his phone instead. Time enough tomorrow to end her tête-à-tête with Samantha. The two girls didn't get to spend a lot of time together, considering Sam was a year and a half older and a senior in the high school. Funny how fate had stepped in and made them best friends considering...

"Looks like I have a welcoming committee," Troy said, pointing at the woman standing on the shore. "She must really need these supplies."

Trace glanced behind him at the crates of fresh produce and then at the curvy brunette waiting below. His stomach flipped and it had nothing to do with Troy's flying aptitude.

Mona.

Mona sighed her relief when the Betsy Boop showed up on the horizon. Troy was about as reliable as they came, but she'd still been worried about her cargo. The diner was low on a number of items, thanks to the recent storms. That was the problem with living on an island, you had to count on the weather in order to survive. The ferries had canceled most of their runs for the week due to rough seas. She'd been lucky to get this short pocket in the weather systems so Troy could do a run for her. Funny thing about bad weather; it was great for business.

The plane circled above Sweetheart Cove a couple of times before coming in for a smooth splashdown on the moody blue-gray water. As she bundled up for her walk down the dock, the door opened, and the grizzled pilot stepped out to secure the moorings. Mona raised her hand in a wave, but Troy had already turned back to the plane and lifted out a dark blue suitcase ahead of another man's descent.

Curious, Mona slowed her pace, allowing the new arrival to get his bearings on semi-solid ground. That is, until she realized *who* had just arrived with her produce—Trace Michaels.

Dammit, it was too late to beat a hasty retreat. She was going to have to buck up and act the responsible businesswoman she'd become, instead of the rebellious teenager who'd had her heart broken thanks to this man.

Troy noticed her first. "Made good time, today. Were you waiting long?"

She smiled at the pilot; aware Trace had stiffened at her appearance. "Not more than five minutes. I owe you a big piece of pie for this, Troy. You saved me from a whole lot of unhappy customers."

"Oh, I can't believe that." Troy grinned, good-naturedly. "Sweet Treats is packed anytime I come to town. I'll need to start phoning for a reservation, soon."

Mona laughed. "You come around back to the kitchen and I'll find you a seat. We'd be lost without you," she added, and was pleased to see him blush.

He glanced from her to Trace, seeming to pick up

on the icy undercurrents. "Well, I'd best get this stock unloaded so you can go about your day." He shook Trace's hand. "Thanks again, Mr. Michaels. I'll tell my Betsy to give you a call."

"You do that." Trace clapped the man on the back and picked up his suitcase to stride toward Mona. "Hi," he said quietly, coming to a stop way too close for comfort.

Even as she took a step back, needing to maintain a physical, as well as mental, distance between them, she couldn't help falling into those eyes. They said the eyes were the window to a person's soul and she'd always believed it until Trace betrayed her and yet denied it the entire time. His electric blue eyes, so startling with dark hair, had convinced her he was telling the truth when it had been nothing but lies. But hey, that was eighteen years ago—she'd gotten over him.

Yeah, right.

"Spending the taxpayer's dime on private vacations, Trace? I'm sure it will go over big with your constituency." Not that they would care, he had half the town in love with him. And how did he manage to get better looking the more he aged, while she... didn't?

"Still packing that chip on your shoulder, I see," he murmured with a slight smile. "Actually, I was on a business trip sanctioned by the board—sorry to disappoint." He glanced over his shoulder as Troy unloaded the first of the heavy crates. "Do you need a hand getting your stock to a vehicle? I assume you brought something larger than that toy car you like to drive?"

He knew what she drove? Well, of course he did. It wasn't like they lived in a huge metropolis. Sweetheart Cove boasted a healthy population of seven thousand which swelled to double the size in the tourist season—or at least, it had.

"I borrowed Jacob's truck, and no thanks. I have someone coming to help me. As a matter of fact, there he is now." She heaved a silent sigh of gratitude as Jason pulled up on his motorbike, the engine giving a throaty growl before he shut it down.

"New boyfriend?" Trace asked, his smile fading.

"New... something," Mona agreed with a brief flare of satisfaction. He may have moved on from their relationship, but there were still dark waters under the bridge. "Sam mentioned Beth was spending the night; are you good with that?" She may harbor complicated emotions for her father, but Beth was a joy to be around. Someday she would have to sit the girls down and have a serious conversation with them. She just hoped they wouldn't hate her after the truth came out.

"Of course, though I think they're planning on the weekend. I'll call Beth in the morning and tell her to come home." Trace glanced at the expensive-looking watch on his wrist. "If you're good here, I better take off. I still have a few hours of paperwork ahead of me." He rubbed the back of his neck, exhaustion darkening his eyes. "Take care of yourself, Mona."

She took a deep breath, inhaling the masculine citrus and pine scent of his body as he brushed by her on the narrow dock. In all the years they'd been apart, her heart still recognized him. It was both thrilling and painful.

She crossed her arms as Jason joined her after a barely-there nod from Trace before he disappeared over the rise. "Thanks for coming."

"No problem," he said, his gaze sharpening on her face. "Was that guy giving you grief? I could—"

Mona shook her head and dropped her arms. "No, it's fine. He's the father of one of my daughter's friends—we were just talking." She steered the conversation away from personal matters. "So, you ready to haul my groceries?"

"Yes, ma'am." He grinned. "That's why you pay me the big bucks."

"Huh, was getting paid part of our agreement? I thought you were my apprentice." She laughed at his expression. "I'm kidding. Okay, let's get this stuff out of the sun, it cost me an arm and a leg."

She couldn't resist one last forbidden look at the shoreline, hoping to catch sight of Trace—but he was gone.

2

Beth sat still, though her insides quivered with suppressed excitement. "Are you done yet? I'm going crazy waiting to see it." *It* referring to the new color and cut Samantha was doing to her hair. She was excited and scared. Excited to see if it made her look older and scared because sooner or later her dad was going to find out and he was going to totally freak.

"Don't move," Sam warned, her scissors snip-snipping Beth's bangs. "Al... most there." She leaned back, teeth nibbling at her lower lip as she concentrated. "Just a little more..."

Clip.

Clip.

Then came the brush and blow-dry and finally, finally they were done. Samantha unclipped the black garbage bag they'd used as a cape and Beth stood, suddenly frightened to look. What if she'd made a mistake? Her head felt so light. She touched the back of her neck and soft strands tickled her fingers, the long hair she'd worn for most of her life gone. For a second, she regretted the impulsive decision to change her looks, but then she thought of Billy Kennedy and how much she wanted him to notice her as something other than *The Geek* and knew she didn't have a choice. Desperate times, and all that.

"Well, are you going to take a look?" Samantha said, grinning like a loon. She grasped Beth's shoulders and spun her to face the large bevel mirror in her mother's bedroom. "You're gorgeous!"

Beth's mouth fell open. Instead of a long, mousy brown mop, her hair was short and... glowing. "It's like a moonbeam," she whispered. The heavy bangs had been replaced with delicate wisps in a variety of lengths that somehow transformed plain blue eyes into deep, mysterious pools of cobalt. She turned her head and gasped at the streak of cotton candy pink flirting with her ear. "You did it." Tears welled and she brushed them away, unwilling to miss a second of this transformation. "I don't know what to say."

"How about you like it, for a start?" Sam rested her chin on Beth's shoulder. "Is it too much?" she asked, worry entering her expressive eyes.

Beth swung around and impulsively hugged her

friend. "Samantha Samuels, you're a genius. It's perfect." Overcome, she twirled out of Sam's arms and danced around the room. "I feel like a new person," she crowed.

Sam flopped onto her mom's bed and sighed. "I am rather gifted, aren't I?" She grinned. "Billy won't be able to take his eyes off you now."

Beth's pulse leapt. She quit twirling to stare at Samantha. "Do you really think so?" She'd never felt like this for a boy before—all jittery and tongue-tied. She could sense him the moment he walked into a room. And he sat right behind her at school.

Sam sat up and nodded. "You should invite him to your birthday bash."

Could she? Her palms turned sweaty just thinking about it. "I don't know..."

"I do," Samantha said. "You didn't risk your father's wrath just to give up now. Come on, Bee, you've gotta try."

A door closed somewhere in the house and Beth's stomach tumbled. "Your mom is home. We better get out of here." She grabbed the garbage bag and frantically tried to corral the pile of hair lying on the floor.

"Don't worry, Mom's cool." Samantha went to the doorway and yelled. "We're up here. Come and see what we've been up to."

Beth found a broom from somewhere and efficiently swept the mess into a dustpan and disposed of it into a trash can under the desk just as Sam's mom appeared.

"What are you two doing in here?" She said, then stumbled to a stop. "Oh, my word." Her hands clasped her cheeks. "Beth?"

Beth gripped the broom handle and wished she could fly out the window. "Yes, ma'am, it's me."

"You look just like your mother," she whispered, reaching out to brush a curl behind her ear. "So pretty."

Sam winked and mouthed, "Told you." Aloud, she said, "Hope it was okay to use your room, Mom. You have the biggest mirror."

"Hmm?" Mona murmured, her fingers busy tweaking Beth's hair. "Of course. As long as you clean up after yourself. Did you talk to your father before getting this done, young lady?" She gave a strand a tug.

Beth wished she was better at fibbing. "No, but to be fair, I *am* almost sixteen."

Mona sighed and took her daughter's seat on the bed. "Honey, you need to call him. It's better if he hears about it from you, instead of someone else." She rubbed her shoulder and grimaced.

Samantha frowned. "Overdoing it again, Mom? I thought that's why you hired the new guy?"

Beth stared at her friend, unused to hearing that tone from her.

"Jason did most of the work. What do you have against him? He's been a tremendous help at the restaurant while I prepare for..." Mona glanced at Beth and stopped, spiking her curiosity.

Her words made Sam scowl. "You may as well tell her, she's going to find out anyway. And I don't have anything against your cook, as long as he does his job."

"Samantha, we'll talk about this later. Right now, I need a long, hot bath, so you girls will have to excuse me." She rose and started toward the ensuite. "Beth, call your dad." She closed the door behind her and left an awkward silence in her wake.

Sam was the first to move. She gathered up her hair styling tools and headed toward the hallway. "Parents, aren't they fun?"

Beth trailed after her, wondering what Mona had been about to say, who Jason was, and if she was about to be grounded for life.

So much fun.

3

Mona closed the door on the girls and leaned her head back to stare at the ceiling. She'd almost let the cat out of the bag before she was ready. She wasn't sure she'd even carry through with it—running against Trace for the mayor's position—was she crazy?

No, she decided, pushing away to start the water running in her luxurious clawfoot bathtub. Someone had to step up to the plate and stand for the integrity of their town. If she was the only one brave enough to campaign against their incumbent mayor, so be it. Sweetheart Cove was her home and she liked it just the way it was. Trace had all these big—costly—ideas to turn the town into a mecca for tourism, which was all well and good, but the price tag would be more than monetary. Change inevitably brought crime, and she wasn't willing to give up her security for a few dollars' worth of income.

She set her phone on the bookstand beside the tub, peeled out of her clothes, and climbed in with a deep sigh. Even with her new cook's help, she was beat. Carrying the stock up from the beach had killed her calves. She lifted the lid off her lavender bath beads and added them to the warm water. Inhaling the luxurious scent, she leaned against the curved backrest and let the bath soak her aches and pains away. She loved this sanctuary Jacob had created for her in the old farmhouse she'd purchased after the restaurant was paid for. Her brother was a talented carpenter whose reputation was growing. He deserved the recognition, he'd earned it. His design for the new health spa had even been featured in *Home* magazine.

Shoot, she was supposed to pick Jane up on her way home. She sat up with a splash and reached for her phone.

Josie picked up on the other end. "Hello, Ms. Mayor."

Mona slapped a wet palm to her forehead. "Josie, I'm so sorry. I had a busy day and then a meeting, and then... No excuses, you should have called."

"And let you run yourself ragged when it wasn't necessary? Jane was a little disappointed, but I assured her you would see her before her birthday on Sunday. You're still coming, right?"

Mona stared at the pale blue wall—cape blue, she'd chosen it herself—and blinked back tears. She was overtired; it had nothing to do with being almost forty and all alone. She was happy Jacob had found someone after the loss of his wife and Jane's paralysis. It's just that sometimes, like now, she felt vulnerable. Lonely. It would pass.

"Mona? Are you still baking the cake? Because if you're busy..."

"No," Mona snapped, her tone bouncing off the wall. She tightened her grip on the phone and lowered her voice. "No, I want to do her cake. It's my pleasure. I can't believe my niece is eight already."

"Jake said the same thing," Josie said. "He wants to give her the moon and the stars but settled for a beautiful locket instead."

That sounded like Jacob. He adored his daughter. He was a good father—like Trace Michaels.

"She'll treasure it. I'm so sorry I messed up your date night, Josie, it totally slipped my mind."

"Small wonder, considering all you have on your plate right now. How's the new cook working out?"

Mona pictured the handsome young man on his Harley. "He's going to break some hearts, I'm afraid, but seems like a hard worker. It's only been a couple of weeks and he's already got the hang of the kitchen. It's a little too early to leave him on his own, but hopefully by the time I need him to take over, he'll be ready."

"This is so exciting. I'm going to burst if I can't tell someone soon."

Mona smiled at her friend's enthusiasm. "Let's see if you still feel that way when I drag you with me on the campaign trail." She swished the water with her toe. "Okay, gotta go. See you Sunday. Hug Jane for me and tell her her aunty is a big dope."

Josies laughed. "I will not. Can't wait to see the mystery cake. Oh, there's Mischief asking for the door. Get some sleep, don't forget, the party's at one. Bye!"

The phone went silent and Mona set it down. She hoped Jane's dog would take well to Sam's gift for her young cousin—a kitten. They still had to pick it up from the pound, but she'd already chosen the one she wanted, a little black and white fur ball. Jacob hadn't looked impressed when they asked if it was all right, but he couldn't say no to his niece, so the cat was getting a home. Samantha had tried the same doe-eyes on her, but she was made of sterner stuff than her brother. Yeah, right.

She'd called the pound the next day and reserved one for her daughter.

They were both pushovers when it came to their kids.

Speaking of which, she hoped Trace wouldn't rake Beth over the coals for her new hairstyle. Turning sixteen was a big deal to a young girl. A time when hormones ruled their lives. She'd been the same way, so she knew what they were going through—and what to watch out for. If she wasn't mistaken, both girls had their eyes on boys. She'd had the talk with Sam a while ago, but a refresher might be in order, awkward or not. Beth was another issue. It wasn't her place to say anything, and Lord knew she didn't want to approach Trace or the girl's mother about it, but someone needed to tell Beth to be careful.

Romance might seem like a fairytale as a child, but the reality was more like a nightmare for a lot of innocent girls.

She should know, she'd been one.

The water had cooled, so she pulled the plug and climbed out to towel-dry and wrap herself in her ratty old robe that she refused to throw away. The ends of her hair had gotten damp, but she was too lazy to bother doing anything with it, leaving the curls to frame her rosy face. Now that she had settled down, Mona's stomach decided to grumble. Maybe the girls had left a slice or two of the pizza she'd ordered for them earlier.

Tightening her belt, she opened the door, walked across the hardwood flooring in her bedroom, and made her way down the hall toward the kitchen. Beth's tear-filled voice made her hesitate, loathe to intrude on a phone conversation. But she couldn't leave her upset, so she entered the room, only to slam to a halt when two sets of identical blue eyes turned her way.

Trace Michaels was in her kitchen.

TRACE STARED at the disheveled woman who'd interrupted the lecture he'd been giving Beth. It had been years since he'd seen anything other than Mona's hard outer shell—he was lost for words. Her pink robe hugged a curvaceous body that set his pulse unaccountably racing as the heady scent of lavender swirled between them like a ghost. He'd bought her bath beads with the same aroma once. It made him wonder what else was the same.

"What are you doing here?" she asked, tightening the tie on her robe, which served to highlight her full breasts.

"He... he said I have to go home," Beth sobbed, her expression mutinous.

Trace frowned at his daughter. "I said it would be *better* if you came home so we could sort this out without disturbing the Samuels'."

"I think that ship has sailed." Mona crossed to the

stove and lifted a copper kettle to test the weight before lighting the gas under the pot. "I'll make us a cup of tea and we can talk. Where's Samantha?"

"She went to her room to give my dad some privacy while he reamed me out," Beth answered, staring at the floor as if she wished it would swallow her whole.

Mona took some multi-colored mugs down from the cupboard and set them on the counter. "My daughter, the diplomat. Well, go and see if she wants to join us, honey, while I have a word with your dad."

Beth barely glanced at her father before bolting from the room as though her legs were on fire.

Mona shook her head and called after her. "Slow down. I don't want to make a trip to the hospital when you fall down those stairs." She waved Trace into a chair. "May as well have a seat. I don't imagine she'll be in a hurry to return."

Trace sat, bemused by how she'd entered the room and taken over. "Are you always this bossy?" The girl he remembered had been shy and introverted.

The kettle whistled and she efficiently moved it off of the hot burner before shutting off the stove, then filled their cups with the steaming liquid before setting the pot down. "Earl Grey good enough for you?" she asked, turning to bring the cups to the table along with a couple of spoons and a cut glass sugar bowl.

"Sure, thanks." He leaned back to give her room.

The hem of her robe brushed his leg and the heat of her body permeated the air, tempting him to drag her into his lap. He frowned. Where did that come from? His and Mona's past was history. A lifetime had elapsed since they'd gone out in school. They were different people now. Older. Wiser.

"I'm guessing Beth didn't ask before getting her hair cut." She took the chair across from him and reached for the sugar bowl. "Milk?"

"Hmm?" he said, his gaze on her gaping robe. "No, this is fine, thanks."

She caught him staring and clutched the flaps together, raising her brow. "Haven't seen a woman's chest for a while, Michaels?"

None like hers. He cleared his throat and concentrated on preparing his tea. "What was wrong with her hair the way it was? She's blond," he added, outraged.

Mona chuckled. "Don't forget the pink streak. I don't know why you're surprised; your ex-wife is blond. It's only natural Beth would want to look like her mom, she's a beautiful woman."

Trace looked up, surprised by her sincerity. It was well known around town that the two women shared a mutual animosity. "Yes, well, she still should have come to me first."

Mona crossed her legs, revealing tanned skin and

pink toenails. "She's a teenager, they act first and think later. Give her a break, it's a good look on her."

Privately, he agreed. Her long hair took a lot of work to keep up and hadn't done much for her delicate features. But, still. If she didn't come to him for advice about something as simple as this, what else would she keep from him? "I need her to trust me," he said.

"I do," Beth replied, entering the kitchen with her friend, Sam, following close behind. "It's my hair, Dad. What's the big deal?"

Samantha slid into the chair next to her mother and took a sip of her tea. "Feel better after your bath?"

Mona leaned over and kissed her temple. "Yes, thank you. Are you going to say hello to Mr. Michaels?"

"Hello," she answered dutifully, then raised a brow at Beth. "Um, I'm sorry?"

Beth frowned and plopped into the other chair. "You don't have anything to apologize for. This is about my father trying to rule my life, it's not your fault." She scowled at her dad.

Trace wavered between frustration and embarrassment. Who was this monster who'd taken over his sweet daughter's body? "We'll save this for home. Did you bring your things?"

"No! I'm not—"

Mona reached over and squeezed Beth's knee and

sent him a warning look. "It's late. Why don't you let her stay the night and I'll bring her home tomorrow? The girls have plans to watch a movie and eat some popcorn, they won't get into anymore trouble. Right, ladies?"

"Yes, Mom." Sam grinned.

"Please, Dad?" Beth begged.

Trace crossed his arms and leaned back. He was outnumbered. Damned if he did, and damned if he didn't. He sighed and nodded. "No more surprises," he warned.

Beth squealed and leapt up to wring his neck in a tight hug. "Thanks, Daddy," she whispered.

Samantha smiled, and Trace felt an odd sense of déjà vu. She reminded him of her mother at that age. "You rock, Mr. Michaels."

The two of them raced out of the room, giggling, and clomped up the stairs like a herd of horses.

Mona turned from watching them go, a warm smile flirting with her lips. "You did good."

His chest swelled at her words and that look in her eyes. "Thanks to you. I owe you one. Raising a kid on your own isn't easy, is it?"

The smile died and he mourned the loss. "No," she agreed, pensively. "It isn't."

He wondered who Sam's dad was, he wanted to kick the guy's ass. Mona was amazing, and Samantha was a great kid. They deserved the father's support, unless... "Is your daughter's father around?" He'd never heard even a rumor of who the man had been. All he remembered was that she'd gotten pregnant not long after they had broken up, but he'd had his hands full with Sally by then—he was ashamed to say—and hadn't kept up with how Mona was managing.

She rose and took her cup to the sink. "It's late," she said. "You should go."

He stared at her reflection in the window. Obviously, he'd touched on a sore subject. He nodded. "Yeah, you're right. Thanks for the tea and the advice." He headed to the door, then hesitated, his hand on the knob. "For what it's worth, I think you're a fantastic mother. Good night, Mona."

He opened the door and left before he said how much he wished things were different between them.

4

Mona flipped the three hot cakes cooking on the stainless-steel grill, cracked two eggs and got them started, and added another layer of bacon in preparation of the next order. She turned to the butcher block counter behind her and chopped onions, peppers, and ham, threw them in a mixing bowl and added three eggs for a Denver omelet. As soon as the pancakes came off, she added the egg mixture and nodded to Jason to drop the toast. Next came the frying eggs. A deft flip with the spatula, count of ten, and done. Add them to the short stack of hot cakes and order up.

"What's next?" she asked her prep cook, handing him the heavy platter.

Jason set the plate on the counter and rang the bell for the server to pick up before leaning closer to the string of orders hanging in front of him. "Meatlovers *x* two, one no cheese. A pig and pickle with soup—" he glanced at the simmering pot on the stove, "and a Rueben with sweet potato fries. Toast is up for the omelet," he added.

Mona completed the next plate and filled the grill with the next orders, then turned to finishing the potato and cheese soup she'd been working on before the late morning rush began. She filled a large mixing bowl with cold water, added salt and pepper and a scoop of flour, whisked the combination into a loose paste and stirred it into the bubbling pot. As soon as it began to thicken, she added four cups of shredded cheddar and smiled as the soup took on the consistency of Velveeta—perfect.

"Soup's ready. Can you fill the crockpot for the girls?" She rinsed out the mixing bowl and returned to the grill in time to add the sizzling sauerkraut and corned beef to the Rueben, flip the sandwiches and plate up the meatlovers, the two of them working like a well-oiled machine.

"Sure thing, boss. I know what I'm having for lunch." He grinned and strode out front for the inset to cauldron the servers used.

Mona lifted the basket of fries from the deep fryer and left them to drain, added dill pickles to the buttered toast Jason had ready, and scooped the

Denver off the grill along with two pieces of bacon. She folded them over the pickles, cut the sandwich diagonally, plated it and set it along with the Rueben on the counter. "Order up," she called and was surprised to see Sam step up to the pickup window. "Hi, baby-girl, what are you doing here?"

Samantha glanced sideways at the grinning Jason and grimaced at the endearment. "I'm filling in for Sara. She called the house, but you'd already left for work. Her sitter is sick, and she couldn't find anyone else."

Mona wasn't sure what she'd done to be blessed with such a thoughtful and kind daughter, but it made her chest swell with pride. Most other teens her age would still be sleeping with a pillow over their heads on a Saturday morning, especially after the late night she'd spent with Beth. Mona had heard them chattering down the hall until the wee hours of the morning but left them to it. Beth needed a little laughter in her life. The child was carrying some deep angst, though if Mona had a mother like hers, she'd be stressed too.

"Where's Beth?"

Sam nestled the soup bowls Jason handed her onto the plates and gathered them up to deliver to her customers. "I left her sleeping. She was worn out, poor kid."

Poor kid. Hard to imagine only two years separated the girls. That and the same biological father, but that was her secret. One she planned on carrying to the grave.

Jason moved aside for Sam to get by with the heavy dishes, but instead of returning to the kitchen he stared after her with a rather intense expression on his handsome face.

Oh, oh. Mona liked Jason, she really did, but he was too old to be looking at her daughter the way a man looks at a woman. Sam had plans. She was going to university in the fall. She was going to make something of herself. A guy like Jason... well, it just wouldn't work, that's all.

"Jason, you can take over in the kitchen. I'm going on a break before the lunch crowd arrives."

He startled and hurried into the room as she removed her apron and hung it on the back door. "Do you need any prep work done, boss?" He used a cleaning rag to sweep the debris from her sandwich making into the disposal cut into the butcher block counter.

"Maybe slice a few more tomatoes and check how much salad we have prepared. If you need me, just shout," she said as she wandered out front. The restaurant was calm now, everyone quiet as they ate their meals and relaxed with full stomachs. Mona loved the hectic rush of a hungry crowd, but it was the satisfied expressions after they finished that filled her heart with joy.

"Mona, another great meal."

"Thanks, Mona. See you on Monday."

"That soup was delicious," Mr. Hayward said, his rheumy blue eyes watering as she sat down at his table. He tugged a faded red hankie from his pocket and rubbed the moisture away. "Darn doctors told me I'd be improved after the eye surgery. They never mentioned I'd be crying like a baby."

Mona smiled and patted his gnarled hand. "It'll get better. Give it time."

He snorted. "I'm too old, time isn't a luxury I can afford."

Maybe not, but he could afford almost anything else. Beth's grandfather was a self-made millionaire, not that you'd know it by his kindly disposition and simple tastes.

"Did you remember to use the eye drops the doctor recommended?" She sat back and turned her cup over when Samantha arrived with the coffee pot. "Yes, please. First one of the day."

"Really?" Sam gazed at her skeptically. "That's not like you."

"I know. Maybe I'm trying to turn over a new leaf," Mona said, shrugging.

Sam touched her forehead. "No fever. Are you sure you're okay, Mom?" She giggled and poured the coffee.

Mona mock frowned. "Everyone's a comedian. You catching a ride home with me after lunch?"

Sam glanced toward the kitchen, then flushed. "Yeah, maybe. I'll see later. Better get back to work, the boss is a stickler."

She moved on to the next table and chatted to the customers, but it was too late, Mona had seen the interest for her Harley-riding cook spring to life in her daughter's eyes. She knew that look and the trouble it could stir. There was no way she was going to sit back and allow Samantha to make the same mistake she had. Now she just had to figure out a way to change the hands of fate.

5

Trace woke early Saturday morning and frowned at his ceiling. He wasn't happy with the way he'd left things with Bethany last night. There was an ever-widening distance between them, and he didn't know what to do to reach her. He missed his girl.

Sighing, he threw back the navy-blue duvet and sat on the edge of the bed, bare legs mottling in the cool air. Beth teased him about being an old woman, but he hated getting overheated while trying to sleep. The house was quiet—too quiet. He'd purchased the Cape Cod cottage overlooking the ocean after separating from Sally and never regretted it. When he won custody of his daughter, the first thing he did was install a pool in the backyard. She loved to swim, and he'd wanted her to have a space she was comfortable in after the upheaval of the divorce. She'd seemed happy.

Now he couldn't tell *how* she felt. He couldn't remember being so contrary when he was a teen—maybe it was a girl thing.

He rubbed his knees, grimacing at the residual ache from the plane trip. Being a tall guy had its disadvantages. Maybe a run would help. He rose and drew his track pants out of the stack of freshly folded laundry he hadn't had the time to put away before his trip to Vancouver.

A few minutes later, he was on the sand inhaling the scent of brine and decomposing kelp that lined the beach. Seagulls wheeled overhead, their shrill squawks an accompaniment to the soft whoosh of the waves. He started out slow, pacing himself in preparation for the five-kilometer loop he planned to travel. Sunrise painted the sky as bright as his daughter's nails in shades of yellow, pink and blue, promising a beautiful day—welcome after the rainy, cold winter they'd endured.

He was nearing the stairs leading up to the road at end of the beach when he noticed a guy running ahead of him. Was that... "Hey, Jake. Wait up."

The other man slowed and turned to jog backwards until he caught up. "Trace. What are you doing out and about so early on a Saturday morning?"

Trace's lips quirked. "I could ask you the same

thing. Don't you have a beautiful new bride to cuddle?"

Jacob's neck reddened. "I'm not supposed to say anything yet, but Josie's pregnant. Morning sickness is giving her hell. She wanted me to '*quit hovering*', her words, so I decided to go for a run."

Trace slapped his shoulder. "Wow, man, congrats. You deserve a second chance more than anyone, truly."

The flush climbed Jake's cheeks. "Should we hug now, or what?" he joked, though Trace could tell he was touched. "After I lost Annie and Jane was injured, I never figured on falling in love again, but Josie... she's special. She makes me happy. Jane, too."

Envy gripped Trace's chest. He reached out and gave his friend a swift man-hug. "A baby, huh?"

Jacob's grin was a mile wide. "Jane's going to have a brother or sister."

"Or both," Trace teased. "Josie might have twins."

"Bite your tongue, man." Jake laughed. "What about you? Are you ever going to give marriage another try?"

Trace shook his head even as a vision of Mona filled his mind as he'd seen her last night in her bathrobe. She'd been pretty as a teenager; but she was beautiful as a woman. "Nah, not me. I learned my lesson the first time." The hard way.

"Well, if you change your mind, Josie has a few

single friends she could introduce to you—as long as you don't scare them off with that scowl," Jacob said pointedly.

"I'm a little old to have my buddy setting me up on a date, however well-meaning." Trace turned his moody gaze toward the water. "With the election coming up in a few months, I'm too busy even if I was interested."

"I'm surprised you're going after it again. Don't get me wrong," Jacob said when Trace shot him a questioning frown. "It's just that you've been mayor for a few years now, I thought you'd be ready to give that stress a pass—spend some time with Beth before she's old enough to head off to university."

Was that why he'd been so discontented lately? It was hard to imagine his baby girl grown and leaving home, but in all reality, it was only a couple of years away. And then he'd be all alone.

A seal popped its head out of the tide, its chocolate brown eyes wise as he stared at Trace. Was he lonely, too? Did he have a family waiting for him, or did he spend his days in an endless loop of searching for food and avoiding predators?

A moment later, the animal was gone, leaving Trace even more restless than before. He took a deep breath and turned to Jake. "My turn for revelations. When Sally got the building permit for her spa, she used my name to get it." He looked for the other shoe to drop in his friend's eyes and didn't have long to wait.

"Isn't that a conflict of interest? Your ex is one for the books." Jake swore under his breath. "I should have never agreed to build the damn place, then you wouldn't be in this mess."

"It was a big project, of course you needed to take it. Besides, she would have just hired a contractor from the mainland if you hadn't agreed to do the job. My ex-wife is a determined woman, she even tricked her father into signing the land over to her."

"You sure know how to pick 'em, dude."

"Don't remind me," Trace muttered. "You know how much the town hates the spa taking up prime waterfront space. I have to find a way to make it up to them and I need the mayoral seat to accomplish that."

"Well, you have our votes and anything else we can do to help, just ask."

"Thanks, Jacob, appreciated." Another couple jogged by, raising their hands in greeting. Not in the mood to make nice with his potential voters, he nodded toward the stairs. "Ready to lose a sprint?"

"Ha," Jake snorted. "In your dreams. Loser buys breakfast?"

Trace wasn't above cheating if it meant free food. He took off, sand spraying beneath his heels. "You're on," he called over his shoulder. If only he could outrun his problems so easily.

"I HEARD an interesting rumor the other day. Are you considering running for mayor?" Mr. Hayward asked, jerking Mona's attention back to her customer.

"You know how people talk," she murmured, frowning. He was losing weight again, the skin around his face loose and sagging like a turkey's neck.

He nodded. "I don't normally listen to gossip, but it came from a credible source." He glanced around the busy room and leaned forward. "I'm an old man, and you certainly have no reason to take my advice, but I hope you'll at least consider what I have to say." He turned his teaspoon over and over as though contemplating his choice of words. When he looked up, his watery blue eyes reminded her of the ocean. "I love my daughter, though I know she can be hard for some people to bear."

Mona couldn't argue with that.

He smiled, his face softening. "She was such a cheerful little girl, always singing and dancing. When my wife died, the light disappeared from our home." He used his hankie to wipe his eyes. "Sally blamed herself. It wasn't her fault, of course—a heart condition, you see—but no one could get through to her. She was the same age when it happened as my Beth, just fifteen." He sighed. "You're probably wondering why I'm telling you all of this; but because of that traumatic event, my daughter is... complex. She may be divorced from her husband, but I can assure you, she won't stand by if someone tries to steal—in her eyes—him or his career. I'm sorry to say, I believe she could be vindictive if crossed." He subsided, withering in his chair.

The roar of the crowd was muted as everything Mona had just heard tumbled in her head like dirty laundry going through a wash cycle. Except, she didn't think she'd be able to remove the stains Sally had left behind. Maybe she'd be better off bowing out of the race before it began. Lord knows, she'd been having second thoughts on the wisdom of going up against Trace anyway. It was better, and safer, if she remained under his radar. But dammit, he'd allowed that spa to be developed, what else was he going to do to ruin their quiet island?

"Mr. Hayward, I appreciate you telling me all of this. I know it must have been hard for you, but I truly believe my platform could win me the election—I have to try." She rose and moved around the table to give him a hug. "I promise I'll attempt to stay out of your daughter's way if you promise to try my blackberry peach pie." She straightened and smiled. "Oh, and by the way, how did you hear I was entering the election anyway? I haven't told more than a handful of people."

"There isn't much that gets by these big ears," he said, tapping one with a finger. "A piece of your homemade pie sounds lovely, thank you, dear. Just remember what I said, will you? I'd hate to see you hurt."

Mona nodded around the lump in her throat. That he would try to protect her from his own daughter was the sweetest thing. She'd often wondered if he'd known what Sally had done to break up her and Trace. But then, if their love had been strong enough, nothing could have come between them. So, Sally had done her a favor. If only her heart would listen to her head.

And speak of the devil; her brother had just walked in with Trace Michaels hot on his heels. She patted Mr. Hayward's shoulder and moved in a fog to the pie shelf, her gaze glued to the two men being ushered to a table by Sam. She was so grateful her daughter took after her side of the family with thick, wavy brown hair and blue-gray eyes. Though, if you knew where to look, there were obvious similarities to her father in the pointed stubbornness of her chin and the brush of freckles across the bridge of her nose. Sometimes, Mona regretted not filling in the father's name on her daughter's birth certificate, lying to Sam and everyone else about who he was, but she'd been young and heartbroken at the time—it had just seemed easier. Now, the omission felt like a quagmire, threatening to drag her under.

"Are you cutting that pie or keeping it all for yourself?" Mona's best friend, Liz, said with a grin.

Mona jerked, and almost flipped the pie plate onto the floor. "You startled me. Where did you come from?"

"No surprise there. I'm not much competition against two of Sweetheart Cove's handsomest men." She waggled her brows suggestively.

"Ew, that's my brother you're ogling," Mona whispered. "I'm telling Josie on you."

Liz shrugged one slim shoulder. "Go ahead. She already knows I adore him. I mean, what's not to like? But I was actually eyeballing our illustrious, *single*, mayor. Do you think I stand a chance?" She spun in a circle, preening like a prom queen.

Mona laughed, though her stomach tightened. "You won't know unless you ask. It's the twenty-first century, girl. If you want Trace Michaels, then go and get him." At least then *she* could quit playing the what-if game.

Liz dropped the pose and batted Mona's arm, once again almost tipping the pie off the shelf. "Ow! What did you do that for?"

"Because you're an idiot," Liz said. She dipped her

finger into some spilled filling and licked it up. "Mmm, this is delicious. What is it?"

"Blackberry peach," Mona answered absently. "Why do you say that?"

Liz sighed and eyed her with big green eyes. "Friends don't poach on a friend's property. You've had a thing for Trace Michaels since high school. And yes, I know that was forever ago, but can you honestly tell me you're over him?"

Mona stared across the room, watching Trace smile up at his daughter while she took his order. Why did life have to be so complicated?

6

By the time Beth dragged herself out of bed, the sun was high in the sky and seemed to frown at her for being lazy. She wasn't usually so tardy, but the argument with her dad had kept her awake half the night. He treated her like a little kid even though she was a grown woman—well, almost. At any rate, if she wanted to color her hair it should be her business. There were plenty of things *he* did that she didn't approve of—talk about a double standard.

She dug through her backpack for the clean clothes she'd grabbed from home and made her way down the hall to the bathroom. The house was silent other than the soft pad of her bare feet on the wood flooring and her heart skipped a beat. Thanks to her choice of horror movies last night she was spooked. She hurried the last few feet to the washroom and locked the door.

Turning on the light, she froze at the strange face in the mirror. A hand went up and tentatively touched pink strands of hair, vivid against the white blond she'd chosen. Her eyes looked huge this morning, dark and mysterious. And the skin she'd always found pale and plain now reminded her of a porcelain doll Grandfather had given her as a child.

But, would it be enough?

In her saner moments, she knew Billy Kennedy wasn't worth the trouble if she had to change who she was for him to take notice, but just once, she wanted to be attractive to guys. To Billy. She really didn't want to be the only one at her sweet sixteen party without a date—how humiliating.

She sighed and started to turn toward the shower when she noticed the pink sticky note tacked to the bottom of the mirror.

Called in to work at the diner. Come for lunch?

A

Guess that explained why the house was so quiet. Everyone was working, except her sorry self. Samantha and her mom were the best. If not for their constant encouragement, Beth didn't know what she would have done. Her mom barely made time for her, and her dad... well, they weren't getting along like they used to. Her shoulders slumped. She hated fighting with him. He'd always been her rock, a safe harbor in a frightening world. She'd never admit it to him, but the divorce had messed with her head. There were times when she'd suffered like a chew toy getting ripped apart between two dogs. And when her mom gave up, walking away from not only her marriage but her kid, Beth's world had turned upside down. Even though she lived with her dad, and he tried his best, she still felt abandoned.

Her phone chimed with an incoming message. She set her clothes on the counter next to the sink and read the note from Sam.

Awake yet?

Just, she answered.

Hurry up, Billy is here—#heartthrob

Beth grinned foolishly even as her cheeks grew hot. *Who is he with?*

His girlfriend—jk. His parents, I think. Just hurry!

K, don't let him leave.

Three dots appeared, then disappeared. Beth held her breath and stared at the screen, willing her friend to reply. Then, finally she did, but it wasn't what Beth wanted to hear.

Your dad is here, too.

Her stomach dropped. So much for that. She couldn't go now. It was bad enough risking Billy's censure, she couldn't handle her dad, as well.

See you when you get home. I don't feel too good.

Dot, dot, dot again, like condemnation pokes in the chest.

You can do this.

Could she? It was a public place, after all. She didn't even need to acknowledge Billy Kennedy. It would be enough for him to see the new her. It had to be.

Be there in ten.

Ready or not, world, here comes the new and improved Beth Michaels.

7

Trace leaned back and enjoyed his coffee as the wash of voices rolled over him in the busy little café. He didn't come to Sweet Treats often, partly because Mona owned it and he still felt like a gangly teenager around her, and partly because his associates generally preferred fancier dining—like the swanky vegan restaurant at the spa. And yes, he realized his ex-wife was playing a one-upmanship game with his ex-girlfriend. That was Sally, she had to be the center of attention.

"Is there anything else I can get you today?" Sam asked, their bill in hand.

"Are you still coming to Jane's party tomorrow?" Jacob asked, pulling a credit card from his wallet.

"Mom and I are looking forward to it," the teen

assured him. "She's decorating the coolest cake, wait until you see it."

That's right, it was Jacob's daughter's birthday. He seemed to remember receiving an invitation for him and Beth a while ago. They'd have to go on a last-minute shopping trip or settle with a gift card—just another way she'd think he'd failed as a father.

"What's with the heavy sigh?" Jake handed over the debit machine and waited for his receipt.

Trace ignored the question to look up at Samantha. "Is Beth still at your house? We have stuff to do today."

She slid a sideways glance at a family sitting across the restaurant before answering. "She was supposed... oh, here she is." She grinned as Beth tugged open the glass door and rushed into the room, then skidded to a stop, her cheeks flushed.

Trace couldn't get over the difference the cut and color had made to her face. His little girl had turned into a young woman before his eyes. He lifted his hand to catch her attention, but her gaze went straight to the family Sam had kept watch over—a shaggy looking boy and his parents. Suspicion raised its ugly head when his daughter fluffed her shortened hair, raised her chin, and strode up to the teen's table as though she owned it. Who was that kid, and what did he mean to Beth?

"Oh, oh. Got your shotgun handy, Dad?" Jacob joked.

"Not funny," Trace growled. "Do you know that boy?" he asked Samantha without taking his gaze off of the stealer-of-his-daughter's-innocence.

"Uhm, I think he's in her class? I gotta go; customers are waiting. See you tomorrow, Uncle Jacob." She scurried away before the interrogation could begin.

He didn't recognize the family, maybe they were tourists? "You know them?" he asked Jake. He was a contractor who had his finger on the pulse of newcomers to town.

"The Kennedys, they moved here a year or two ago. The dad is a vet. I'm surprised you haven't met him yet." Jake smirked over the rim of his cup. Easy for him to do, his daughter was only eight.

Trace started to rise, planning on introducing himself as Sweetheart Cove's influential mayor, but a feminine hand planted itself on his shoulder and forced him back to his seat. He frowned as Mona moved to block his view of the other table.

"Quit intimidating my customers, I don't like it," she said, arms crossed under full breasts.

As disgruntled as he was, his pulse still kicked up at her proximity. "You need a dress code here, that kid over there looks like a hoodlum."

Amusement made her pretty eyes sparkle. "Then I'd have to kick you two out, as well." She stared pointedly at their track clothes. "Still running from your problems, Michaels?"

"Mo," her brother warned. "Play nice."

Trace rubbed his chest where her words had stabbed him. "I deserved it," he told his friend. "Sorry," he said to Mona—for now and for the past.

She hesitated, her face clouding, then she nodded and took a seat. "It's probably not my place to say anything, but if you keep coming down so hard on that girl, she's going to close herself off from you. I don't think that's what you want."

Trace frowned, but had to acknowledge her words. How was he supposed to protect Beth if he wasn't allowed to do anything? Was it too late to send her to an all-girls school?

A moment later, Beth was heading their way with stars in her eyes. "Hi, Dad, are you ready to go? I need to clean my room."

Jake laughed, then coughed into his hand, eyes watering. "See you at the party, Jane can't wait."

Beth looked confused, her mind obviously on something—or someone—else. She made a quick recovery though. "Oh, right. Dad, we have to go shopping. I know exactly what I want to get her." She grinned, all sunshine and rainbows while a storm cloud hovered over Trace's head.

The other family funneled past them on their way

out the door and the kid had the temerity to wink at Beth. Trace saw red and would have risen, if not for Mona's fingers digging into his thigh.

She shot him a glare, then smiled at the Kennedys. "Thank you for stopping by, come back anytime."

Mrs. Kennedy put her hand on her son's shoulder, slowing him down. He obliged without argument, standing at her side while the father continued on out the door. "This was Billy's idea. He said a friend at school recommended the café to him." She smiled at Beth. "I'm glad we came; the meal and the service were perfect."

Billy swept shaggy bangs off his forehead and squinted at Beth from half-closed eyes—the punk. "See you at school?"

Beth turned ketchup red. "Sure," she mumbled.

The mother nodded at Mona and then they moved off, leaving a weighty silence in their wake.

Mona patted Trace's leg and let him go. "Well, I better get back to work before they fire me," she joked, rising.

Beth gave her a surprising hug. "Thanks for letting me stay over," she mumbled.

Mona kissed her brow. "Our house is your house. The hair looks even better today, doesn't it, guys?" She shot them an agree-with-me-or-else look.

Jacob nodded willingly. "It suits you," he agreed. "Though I liked your old hair, too."

Way to walk the line, buddy. Trace raised his brow and Jake shrugged as though to say, "Women, what can you do?"

"Dad, do you like my hair?" Beth's voice trembled slightly, though she looked him in the eye.

What could he say? "It's beautiful, honey. It makes you seem all grown up." His hand flexed on his leg, wishing Mona's fingers were still there.

Beth's smile was worth the angst. "That's because I am, Dad. I can even go out on a date soon. You said when I turned sixteen, right?"

Aw, shit. That was before he realized it could actually happen. This island wasn't big enough for him and Beth's potential suitors. It wouldn't be good for the mayor to land in jail.

8

Mona cursed the rain, juggling keys and the pink pastry box containing her niece's birthday cake while trying to open the car door. On the other side of the vehicle, Sam was doing the same with a bulky cat carrier, bags of food and litter, and a gift-wrapped box filled with half the cat toys from the pet store. The caged kitten yowled her displeasure, not impressed with the trap she found herself in.

Finally, they managed to get settled without losing cake or cat and she sighed her relief. "Ready, kiddo?" She glanced in the backseat to check on their precious cargo. "I hope Jane likes her surprise."

Sam did up her seatbelt and stared pointedly until Mona reached for hers before answering. "Jane's best friend is diabetic, Mom. A unicorn means a perfect blood glucose reading. She's going to love the cake."

Mona's heart squeezed. Her niece had been through a rough couple of years with the loss of her mother in the car accident and her subsequent paralysis. She would do just about anything for that little girl. "Don't forget the cat. Uncle Jacob will be thrilled." She grinned, picturing her dour brother chasing the little monster around his fancy house.

"Is Jason coming to the party?" Sam casually brushed a speck of non-existent lint from her pleated skirt.

Mona frowned at her daughter's bent head. "To an eight-year old's birthday party? I don't think that's really Jason's speed, but you never know." She started the car and played with the vents until Samantha glanced up. "Do you have something you'd like to tell me?" she said calmly while inside a dozen angry hornets buzzed in her ears. Jason was too... everything for her daughter. He was five years older (or so his resume stated), rough around the edges, hadn't finished school, rode a motorcycle, and had a *tattoo.* She knew because she'd seen it peeking out from the neck of a ragged t-shirt he'd worn when he came to help her on the docks. Not that she was judging him. He seemed like a nice kid and had a good work ethic. But, and it was a big but, he was not the right guy for Samantha to get attached to—she'd only get hurt.

"No! Jeez, Mom." Sam flounced back in her seat

and stared out the windshield. "We're just friends, okay? I thought it would be nice to have someone there that was closer to my age, that's all."

"Well, no problem then," Mona replied, backing out of the driveway and gunning it down the street. "Josie will be there, and you get along fine with her." It was true that Jacob's new wife was ten years younger than him, but she'd infused so much light and love into their home that the age difference didn't seem to matter.

She still didn't want that for Samantha though. Her daughter was going places. Her grades were excellent, and she was already sending out applications to colleges and universities across the country. Mona was determined Samantha would get the opportunities that she'd missed out on because of a love affair with the wrong boy. History was *not* going to get a chance to repeat itself.

The rest of the drive was completed in stony silence with Sam pouting in the corner and Mona mentally girding her loins for the upcoming confrontation with Trace. She should have told him yesterday about her decision to run against him. It would have been easier in a full restaurant where he couldn't create a scene, but he deserved to know and she'd rather it came from her than say... his ex-wife. Just thinking about that woman and how she took advantage of her kind-hearted father got Mona's back up. Poor Mr. Hayward didn't deserve the shrew that was his daughter.

The climb up the mountain from town was spectacular. Small wonder Jacob had bought land up here. The rain had stopped and now the trees glittered under bright sunshine while the ocean played peek-a-boo far below them and eagles soared overhead. The drive was private, a slash of gray asphalt among the verdant greens of the forest floor. The house was modern, sleek and stylish with a million-dollar view overlooking the strait below. He'd built it for his first wife and almost sold it after her death, but Josie had convinced him to keep it as a legacy for Jane and Mona would be forever grateful to her for that.

They pulled in behind a shiny sedan and the front door of the house flew open. Mischief bounded out, living up to his name by racing around the vehicles barking like he was spring-loaded, with Jane following close behind in her electric wheelchair.

"Aunty, Aunty," Mona heard as she stepped out of the car. "Everyone is here and I was worried you wouldn't make it, but Daddy said, 'Quit worrying, you know your aunt is always running late,' and he was right, because you are," she ended in a breathless rush, grinning ear to ear.

Mona laughed and leaned down to give her niece a

warm squeeze, inhaling the strawberry shampoo she favored. “Well, we’re here now, so the party can start,” she said, spying her brother and Josie in the doorway. “I hear someone turned seven today?”

“Aunty.” The munchkin laughed. “I’m eight now. Did you forget?”

Mona pretended to look surprised. Even though they played this same game at all of her birthdays, it never got old. “Really?” she said. “That could be a problem then, I only brought enough candles for seven.” She took a step back to her car. “I’ll be right back, *if* I can find a store to sell me one candle.”

Jane shrieked and the dog went ballistic, which in turn caused the kitten that Sam had just removed from the backseat to bounce so hard it knocked the carrier out of her arms. The basket hit the ground, popped open, and a streak of gray raced for the woods with Mischief hot on its trail.

Trace picked his way over decomposing logs blanketed in a thick green coat of moss and pushed aside towering ferns as high as his thighs in a futile effort to find the missing kitten. Mona marched along a few feet away, waving her cell phone’s flashlight from side to side like a homing beacon—one the scared cat ignored.

Further down the ridge, Jacob and Josie worked a grid pattern with Samantha and Jason (who'd arrived at the party against Mona's wishes) while Beth waited at the house with a distraught Jane and her friends. Mischief had been banished to his kennel with his tail between his legs. Obviously, he knew he'd made a mistake in his choice of chew toys.

"This is impossible." Mona stopped and clamped her hands onto shapely hips. "That kitten is probably halfway to town by now."

Trace privately agreed with her, but Jane's woebegone face wouldn't let him give up the search. "Come on, Samuels. I never took you for a quitter." He grinned as her eyes flashed and she began to beat the bushes around her legs. "Are you trying to rescue that cat or do it physical injury?"

"Do I get a choice?" She grumbled. "I'm not a fan of bugs, okay? Who knows what's living in these woods? Slugs and spiders and earwigs are not my friend, so go away," she warned any would-be creepy-crawlies.

Trace chuckled.

"What are you laughing about?" Mona swatted the air around her head. "Oh, Lord, I think I just walked through a giant spider web."

"They're more scared of you than you are of them."

He took pity on her and removed his jacket so she could use it to cover her hair. "Here, use this."

She accepted the coat with a grudging thanks. "I'm not really the outdoorsy type," she murmured.

"No kidding." Trace helped situate the material to protect her face and neck, holding the lapels against her cheeks. "Here I was, thinking you were invincible."

Whiskey brown eyes stared up at him. "My heart bleeds, Trace. Want to ask me how I know?"

Regret closed his throat. He'd made so many mistakes, but none worse than what he'd done to this woman. "Mona," he croaked. "You're killing me here."

A sad smile tipped her lips. "Sorry, I guess I'm feeling sentimental today. Ignore me."

He shook his head and kissed her brow. "Not possible, sweetheart. You're pretty much unforgettable." Immediately, he could tell he'd said the wrong thing. She stiffened in the circle of his arms and took a step back, breaking contact.

"Funny, that's not the impression I got at all." She tossed his jacket at him, narrowly missing his face. "Seems to me, the moment you set eyes on Sally Hayward, I became old news." She lifted her chin. "Am I missing anything?"

Damn, she was beautiful when she was mad—or aroused. But she was also wrong. Sally had turned his head, sure. He'd been a hot-blooded teen and she'd been willing, but he would never have cheated on Mona if he knew then what he knew now. The trick would be to convince her to give him another chance. Going by her expression at the moment, that would be approximately... never.

"There's more to the story, things you should know, but—" He glanced around the forest, hearing the faint calls from the others searching for the kitten. "Now is not the time. Just..." he grasped her arm when she would have turned away, "give me a chance?"

She stared down at his hand, her jaw clenched. "I need you to let go of me," she gritted.

He released her, stunned by the hurt and anger he saw in her eyes. "Mona, talk to me."

Instead, she grabbed his wrist and lifted it up so he couldn't avoid seeing the gold band on his ring finger. "Still up to your old games, Trace?" She choked out a laugh. "You'd think I'd learn, wouldn't you?"

She dropped his arm like it was one of those bugs she was so worried about and wanted to stomp into the ground. "Just stay away from Sam and me. We don't need you. We never have."

Before he could figure out what that was supposed to mean, she took off toward the house as though her tail was on fire. He stared after her, cursing her hot temper and his idiocy in never removing his wedding ring. It hadn't meant anything to him in a long time, but he thought maybe Beth took some comfort from the knowledge her parents had once cared for one another. He tugged it off and dropped the warm metal in his pocket—too little, too late.

"Hey, Trace," Sam called, appearing with that kid from the docks. "Look, we found the kitten." She held the bedraggled cat in the air. "Where's Mom?"

Trace glanced hard at the boy's arm around her waist before forcing a smile. "She was tired, so she headed back to the house."

Sam nodded. "She's been working really hard since she decided to run for mayor—oops! I wasn't supposed to say anything until she's ready to make the announcement." She covered her mouth with one hand, her eyes big.

Dazed, Trace rubbed his chest, feeling as though he'd had the rug pulled out from under him. "Don't worry, I won't say anything," he mumbled. "You better get that kitten up to Jane before she thinks her party is a disaster."

Sam looked at him, concerned. "Are you, uhm, okay?"

Depends. Was it possible to survive a direct hit to the solar plexus? She'd been right there, too. Why hadn't she told him what she'd planned? Dammit, if she was trying to ruin his life for revenge, Mona Samuels was going to have a war on her hands.

9

Beth pretended to have a good time at Jane's party (thanks to Sam finding the kitten) but it was impossible not to notice the strain between her dad and Mona. Ever since they'd returned from the woods—separately—Mona had gone out of her way to avoid him while his scowl was enough to scare all but the bravest away.

She wished Billy was here. Samantha and Jason were helping Josie in the kitchen, Jacob was talking to her dad, and by the look on his face it wasn't a pleasant conversation, while Mona helped Jane with the new kitten. She could join them, but it felt like she'd be betraying her dad to hang out with the enemy, so to speak.

Sighing, she walked over to her father, intending to

ask him if he'd like a drink. Instead, she stumbled into a heated argument.

"If you knew, you should have told me—we're supposed to be friends," her dad growled.

Jacob snorted. "In the first place, I wasn't sure she was going through with it, and second, she's my sister. Give me a break, man. If I could have mentioned it, I would have."

Beth's heart battered her chest. The animosity between the men was almost a physical presence. She'd never seen her dad so riled. She tucked her hand in his and received a comforting squeeze.

"Everything okay, Dad?"

He glanced down at her, his expression grim. "Just a misunderstanding, honey. Don't worry about it." His gaze migrated across the room. "Looks like Jane loves her new kitten."

Beth frowned. "I'm not a kid anymore, you can quit hiding things from me." Like when her mother had given her up without a fight.

He tucked her under his arm and kissed the top of her head. "You'll always be my baby girl, no matter how old and decrepit you become." He smiled and she was too relieved to see the tension dissipate to remain frustrated.

"Gee, thanks, Dad. Seriously, what's going on?

Mona looked upset when she came in. Does this have something to do with her?"

"Josie probably needs a hand, so I'll leave you to it," Jacob said. He gave his friend a warning look, then strode over to hug Jane and have a word with Mona.

Her dad's gaze followed them, his expression melancholy, and suddenly Beth got it. "Dad, do you *like* Mona?" It seemed so obvious now, the way he always watched her and the odd tension between them whenever they were close. The snarky comments took on another context from her new perspective. Images of their blended families filled her head. Sam would be her sister, Jane a cousin. Aunts and uncles; a step-mother. A family. It had been just her and her dad for so long, it would be a dream come true if she could figure out a way to bring them together.

He startled and took her arm to lead her over to the floor-to-ceiling picture window. When they were out of earshot, he said, "We've known each other for years, of course I like her."

He wasn't going to confide in her. That was okay. There was more than one way to get the deets. "She's pretty, isn't she? I love her eyes, and she's such a great mom. Sam is so lucky."

Instead of getting him to confess his undying love, Beth got worried dad. "Honey, you know you can tell me anything, right? And your mom isn't very far away..."

Maybe not, but as far as she was concerned Sally (she preferred not to be called Mom) could be on the other side of the world.

"This isn't about me, Dad. Something is going on between you and Mona and I want to know what it is."

For a long moment, they stared outside at the sweeping vista of field and forest with the navy-blue ocean rising up to meet baby-blue sky. Gulls whirled overhead and high above them, a lone eagle soared amongst the clouds.

"Did you know Mona and I... dated in high school?" he said, his voice soft and filled with memories.

Beth's mouth dropped. *Holy cow!* That explained the familiarity between them. Maybe she was wrong, and they weren't attracted to each other. Or maybe they were, and the past was holding them back from giving their love a second chance. Oh, man, she needed to talk to Samantha, ASAP!

"Uhm, no?" she whispered, realizing she hadn't answered. "How long did you... *date*?" Talk about your over-used euphemisms.

He glanced at her, amusement sparking in his eyes. "A while. My point is we have a long history, long enough that if she was to make a life-changing decision that could directly impact our lives, it would be incumbent on her to tell me—don't you think?"

She tried to follow his logic, but without more information it quickly became a mind-maze and she was lost. "What do you mean? What life-changing decision, and what do *we* have to do with it?"

He sighed again and turned back to the window, his shoulders hunched. "Mona has decided, in all her infinite wisdom, to run against me in the mayoral campaign."

"But..." How could she? Beth swung around to gaze upon the traitor in their midst. Never mind the restaurant, what about Sam and her? This would put them on opposite sides in what could turn out to be a nasty battle. "She can't."

"Unfortunately, she can," her dad muttered. "I just don't understand why."

Neither did Beth, but she was going to find out.

"Mona," she called, ignoring her dad's hissed command to stop. "Are you truly going up against my dad for mayor? How could you?"

The room was so silent they could hear the ticking of Josie's prized cuckoo clock in the kitchen. All eyes were trained on her and her father like they were the main act at an illusionist's show, but Beth didn't care. These people were like family to her—if they'd betrayed him… well, they'd betrayed her, too. And that hurt.

Her dad wrapped an arm over her shoulders and gave her a hug, in effect providing a united front. "Jane, I'm sorry to ruin your party, but I think Beth and I should go."

Jacob stood in the kitchen doorway with Jason, their expressions grim.

Mona and Samantha stared at them as though they couldn't understand how anyone could be less than pleased by the big news.

Mona was the first to speak. "Don't go, this is my fault. I should have known it wouldn't stay a secret for long, nothing does in this town." Her smile was bitter. "I didn't realize it would be such a big deal."

Beth's dad growled something under his breath while Jacob raised a hand for calm. "Let's all take a deep breath and sit down to talk, okay?" He waited until he received a reluctant nod from everyone. "But not until we celebrate my girl's birthday with some cake. Are you ready to sing?"

As everyone broke into a discordant rendition of the song, Beth wondered if they'd ever find harmony again.

10

A couple of hours later, after orange creamsicle unicorn cake, vanilla ice cream, and gift opening, the excitement had died down. Josie said goodbye to their guests, then took Jane off to bed, dog and cat following behind the wheelchair. Jason was next to leave, promising to open the café in the morning.

Good thing, because after this day was over, Mona planned to bury her head under her pillow and not come out until the election was over. She'd done some idiotic things in her life, but this took the cake.

Jacob leaned back in his chair and patted his flat stomach. "That cake was delicious, sis. You outdid yourself."

Sam forked the last bite on the plate into her mouth and closed her eyes in bliss. "I wonder if Jane would mind if I take the leftovers." She grinned.

"Beth's birthday is in a couple of weeks. You can have more cake then," Mona admonished.

Beth glanced sideways at her dad, then lifted her chin. "Will you make my cake, Mona?"

"She's probably too—"

"Of course, honey," Mona interrupted him with a sharp look. "Any thoughts on what you want?"

Beth nodded. "I was kind of thinking... the BTS logo?"

Mona's brows rose. She looked to Samantha for clarity. "BTS?"

Sam gave a long-suffering sigh. "The pop band, Mom. They're only like world famous."

"Whatever happened to groups with real names, like The Rolling Stones or Rush?"

"I think they went out with Y2K," her brother murmured, eyes flashing his amusement.

"Ha, you're older than me. Are you saying you've heard of this band?" Mona pointed her fork at Jacob, aware of Trace's smile as he listened to their nonsensical banter.

"The question is, hasn't everyone?" Trace interjected. "They were even on Ellen."

Oh, well then. "Okay, oh wise one, what does their logo look like?" Mona crossed her arms and prepared to be entertained.

"Already ahead of you," he said, waving his phone

in the air. "*A set of doors meant to represent moving from the past to a better future,*" he read from the screen. His gaze softened on his daughter's bowed head. "I think it's perfect."

Beth looked up at his words, her young face filled with hope. "Does that mean you're going to let me take driving lessons?"

Trace grimaced. "Let's worry about that *after* the party, okay?"

As with most teenagers, she heard the part she wanted to hear. "Oh, thank you, Daddy." She jumped up to give him a hug. Caught off guard, Trace's expression went from surprise to tenderness as he enfolded his daughter in his arms, deflating much of Mona's animosity. They may be worlds apart on the political front, but there was no denying Trace was a good father.

Her gaze went to her own girl and her heart clenched. Sam was watching the father-daughter duo with such longing it hurt. What she'd done wasn't fair to Samantha or to Trace, but it was too late to change it now.

If only...

"Well, Jane and her menagerie are settled but she was hoping you and Beth could read her a story before bedtime," Josie said to Sam as she reentered the dining room. "Sorry, Dad, you've been ousted by girl power."

She looped her arms around Jacob's neck and gave him a commiserating kiss on the cheek.

Sam grinned and rose. "Don't worry, Uncle, your stories are still the best. Come on, Beth. Let's see if we can come up with something scary for the munchkin. Joking," she added with a laugh at Jacob's mock-threatening expression.

The room was quiet after they left, the vitality gone. Mona shifted in her seat, aware that she owed not just her family, but Trace an explanation. "Any more coffee left?" she asked Josie, searching for excuses to put off the inevitable.

"I made a fresh pot after dinner," Josie said, heading for the kitchen. "I figured we might need it after that meal." On her way out, she glanced over her shoulder with a raised brow as though to say, *there's your opening, now what are you going to do with it?*

Mona chuckled at the not-so-subtle hint. Obviously, the time had arrived to make her announcement. She kept her gaze focused on the family portrait hanging on the wall across from her. Jacob stood tall and proud in front of his bride, while Josie's face was effervescent, filled with love for her new husband. Jane, lovely in a butter-soft satin dress, sat in her rose and ribbon decorated wheelchair with a smile brighter than the sparkling blue waves behind them. That was the reason she'd taken on this challenge, so their community could continue to have warm and *safe* moments like her brother's beach wedding.

She'd fight tooth and nail for her family's security, and if that meant taking on Trace Michaels, so be it.

"I guess the news is out, so it's no surprise I've decided to run for mayor." She turned to Trace, feeling the magnetic pull of his eyes. "I want you to know I've always stood behind your mandates—at least until last year when you allowed land that should have been turned into a park become a high-end spa for your wife's rich guests. Guests that bring garbage and less than savory people to the island. And don't get me started on the carbon emissions from all the private float planes taking off and landing on our small dock—a dock nowhere big enough to handle that kind of commerce. It's disrupting local businesses and making it a full-time job for our authorities to keep up with the rise in crime. I want her gone." She took a deep breath, her pulse pounding at the red fingers of anger suffusing Trace's cheeks.

"Wow, sis. Say it like it is, why don't you." Jacob whistled.

She flushed but didn't back down. "You know I'm right, Jake. Just last month your work truck was burglarized, and you lost half of your tools. Liz told me she had a break-in at the flower shop. Whoever it was left the cooler open, destroying hundreds of dollars in fresh flowers, and emptied the till. We never had issues like this before the spa opened."

Josie returned in time to overhear and turned to her husband in concern. "Why didn't you tell me you were robbed? How horrible."

Jacob stood to take her in his arms and mouthed, *thanks a lot*, to Mona. "I had insurance coverage, babe, I didn't want to worry you."

She slapped his arm—hard. "We're a team, Jacob Samuels. Don't hide things from me, I don't like it."

He grimaced. "Yes, ma'am. Let's go into the kitchen so I can properly apologize." He took her hand and kissed the palm, leading her away without a backwards look.

Mona fanned her face, suddenly warm. "Well," she murmured. "I didn't mean to get him into trouble."

Trace got up to pour the coffee Josie had left on the side table. "He's a big boy, I wouldn't worry about it." He pulled out the chair next to hers and took a seat. "You should have come to me with your concerns, Mona. And by the way, Sally is my ex-wife. We divorced over three years ago, she has nothing to do with my present life, okay?"

His eyes, those gorgeous blue orbs she'd dreamed of, stared at her with such a deep intensity butterflies took flight in her tummy. She hadn't been this close to Trace in years. Her vision blurred, caught in a time warp between past and present. He smelled the same, an intoxicating mix of pine and sun and ocean breezes. She remembered the night she'd given him her virginity, the night she fell in love.

"Do you ever go back to Sunset Beach," she asked, half afraid of what his answer might be. If he'd ever taken...

"No," he answered, his voice rumbling over her emotions the way his feet had done to her heart. "Do you?"

Her laugh lacked humor. "Back to my biggest mistake? Not likely." She was being deliberately cruel but couldn't help it. He'd ruined her for anyone else that summer—it wasn't fair.

He tipped her chin up, his thumb close to her bottom lip, causing those butterflies to beat themselves against the walls of her chest. "I still remember everything about that night. You wore a pretty white dress and your hair was done up in a ponytail. I wanted to wrap my hand in it and kiss you senseless."

"I think you did." She smiled, caught up in the memories he wove like a master tailor. "I knew what you were up to with that blanket and picnic hamper, but I didn't care. The great Trace Michaels wanted *me* —I could barely believe it was happening."

He brushed his thumb over her lip, igniting the embers of a long-ago fire. "We were good together,

Mona. I'm sorrier than you can ever know that I screwed it up."

She yanked free, angry and embarrassed at her weakness. "Screwed Sally, you mean? You were a free agent, it didn't matter." Or so she'd spent the next ten years trying to convince herself. "It's all water under the bridge now anyway. I'd sooner stick to the subject at hand. What are you going to do about the spa?"

His dark brows drew together, and he opened his mouth as though he had something to say, before letting it snap shut. Instead, he leaned back, crossed his leg over his knee, and took a sip of his coffee before eyeing her over the rim of the cup. "I think I'll leave the politics for the debate table. After all, you've known for some time who your opponent would be, I need time to study mine." He tipped his cup at her and winked.

11

Mona pounded the stake into the ground, wishing it was Trace's head on a pike. Every time she thought about the evening of Jane's birthday, her blood pressure rose. What did he think he was doing, bringing up ancient history, getting her all hot and bothered, then trying to apologize? They were way past the place where an apology was going to solve their issues. Too little, too late.

Bam, bam. There was something satisfying about using a hammer to smash a piece of wood, the repercussions vibrating up her arm like a string of curse words. No wonder her brother had become a carpenter. It was a great stress-reducer. Maybe *Sally* could introduce it at the spa.

Bam.

Bam.

Okay, if she were being honest, jealousy played a tiny—miniscule really—part in her determination to rid the island of that... that building down there. She glared at the offending piece of architecture. She couldn't even call it ugly. Jacob had designed the structure, it was a work of art, really. Too bad it belonged to the biggest pain in her...

"Excuse me, you can't put that there," a nasally voice squawked from behind her.

Tightening her grip on the hammer, Mona turned to face the object of her revulsion. "It's public property, Sally. I have as much right to advertise as you do." She used the hammer to point at the giant billboard with the blond bimbo's face plastered on one side while the other extoled the virtues of a cleaner, healthier lifestyle.

Sally glared at her from the driver's seat of her fancy sports car. Blood-red fingernails tap-tapped the expensive paint where they rested on the windowsill. The convertible top was down, showing off snow-white leather upholstery and a carbon fiber dash. The queen bee wore a floppy white beach hat and Hollywood-style sunglasses that hid her eyes, but Mona didn't need to see them to read her expression. The pinched lips—red to match her nails—and clenched jaw gave the story away. Ms. Michaels wasn't happy.

Good.

"Mona? I didn't recognize you in those... clothes." Sally let her gaze drop from Mona's baggy sweatshirt down to her Lululemon leggings with their cute flower print, and paint-splattered runners.

Mona refrained, barely, from tugging the waistband of her sweater over her curvy hips. "These old things? I couldn't see the sense in getting dressed up to do manual labor. Besides, I knew I'd be hot and sweaty by the time I was done. Not all of us can ride around in style." She smiled woman-to-woman.

"Yes, well, I would expect a businesswoman on the road to a political career to take more care with her image, but maybe that's just me. At any rate," she waved her queenly fingers at Mona's campaign poster, "good luck." She didn't say, *you're going to need it*, but she may as well have.

"I appreciate the vote of confidence," Mona said, her sarcasm hitting the mark as Sally's fingers turned white where she gripped the steering wheel. "But luck won't win me the chair—hard work will." Not that the other woman knew what that was. Between her daddy and Trace, Mona doubted whether she'd ever had to lift a finger in her life.

"If you say so," Sally replied. "No more poster boards or I'll go to the city council- they're an eyesore."

With that she roared off, floppy hat waving in the breeze.

Left on her own again, Mona's shoulders curled in defeat. She hated confrontations, and this one left a bad taste in her mouth. Or maybe that was Sally. The woman definitely rubbed her the wrong way. Even in school, she'd been the typical prom queen, while Mona and her few friends hung out in the background wishing they were her. That changed for Mona the night she'd caught Sally and Trace together, but the not-good-enough feeling dogged her steps to this day.

Sighing, she turned to take down the offending poster only to freeze at the sight of Trace leaning on the post under Sally's billboard like James Dean in a business suit.

"How long have you been standing there?" she demanded.

He straightened and walked toward her, lean and dangerous. "Long enough to overhear you and Sally butting heads."

Great. Now she was going to get a lecture from him on his ex-wife. Where was that pike?

Trace wasn't sure if he should hug Mona or shake her. Why she would decide to virtually flip her middle finger at Sally by placing those ads in front of her place of business was anyone's guess. The damn woman liked to court trouble.

"I heard a rumor my competition was working her cute little butt off pounding signs and had to come out to see it for myself. Imagine my surprise when I find said butt in about the only place on the island bound to raise a stink. Why would that be, I wonder?"

"You do realize I'm armed, right?" Mona lifted her hammer and pointed the handle at him. "Sexist comments are *so* unattractive."

He stumbled to a halt, his Italian loafers not meant for roaming hills. "Whoa, that wasn't my intention. I have the utmost respect for women—ask anyone." He grinned, inviting her to relax.

She frowned but let the hammer fall to the sandy soil with a dull thunk. "I have no doubt." She eyed his suit and tie, then glanced down at her own casual clothes. "I assume you have a reason for stalking me?"

He'd forgotten how prickly she was in the morning. "I had a break between meetings and decided it was too nice to stay indoors, thought maybe you might like to join me for coffee."

The frown deepened. "What are you really up to, Michaels? We aren't exactly bosom buddies."

His gaze dropped to her sweatshirt with the slogan,

Bite Me, written across her chest and his blood heated. If she were willing, he was ready. Unfortunately, her moody brown eyes didn't say, *sweep me off my feet*. More like, *come closer and I'll clobber you*. The grin flirting with his lips became a full-blown smile. "I've missed you, sweetheart."

Mona startled, freckles standing out with her temper. "Don't call me that. You gave up the right a long time ago."

He sobered. "I'm not trying to fight, Mona, only invite you to a cup of coffee." He'd hurt her. He'd known and regretted it, but still, her bitterness seemed over the top for a teenage romance gone wrong. Before he could question her, she turned away and distracted him by bending over to pick up the hammer. A couple of cars zoomed by honking and they both put on their public faces to smile and wave.

When they were alone, Mona crossed her arms. "Coffee's a bad idea, Trace. We have too much history. Besides, I'm not really dressed for a restaurant."

So, it wasn't exactly a no. She just needed convincing.

"I need your advice," he said.

She gazed at him skeptically. "You've run two terms as mayor, I'm pretty sure you know what you're doing."

Kind of a back-handed compliment but he'd take it.

"Thanks, I appreciate the support." She threatened him with the hammer again, so he hurried to add, "but this is about Beth. I could really use a woman's insight."

She hesitated, then sighed. "Fine, you win. Where do you want to go?"

Anywhere, as long as it's with you. "Broadmoor Park? It's nearby and there's a drive-through coffee place on the way." He held his breath until she nodded.

"I suppose I could use a drink. Meet you there? Where are you parked?"

It was almost as though she didn't want to be stuck in a car with him. "I walked," he fibbed. "I'll catch a lift with you." He kept his smirk to himself at her obvious frustration.

"Yeah, sure. I'm parked around the bend. Let's go then, I have work to do." She gathered a stack of posters and left him to grab the rest.

He took a moment to enjoy her gentle sway as she walked down the hill, then undid his suit jacket and bent to the job she'd given him. He'd parked his vehicle in the spa's lot, intending to stop in and question Sally about her customer base, until he'd seen Mona on top of the hill. He had a feeling she wouldn't wait for an explanation if she knew, so he'd lied about walking. Hopefully, it didn't come back to bite him on the ass.

The ride to the park was made mostly in silence

other than his choice of coffee at the drive-through window. Trace figured he was better off giving her some space, but he was hyper-aware of every breath she took, the brush of her hand against his leg as she changed gears, the sweet, clean scent of her hair. He shifted uncomfortably.

She handed him his drink and shot him a glance. "Scratchy suit?"

Something itched, but it wasn't his clothes. "Something like that," he murmured, accepting the cup.

She smirked, thanked the server, and placed her cup in a holder. "Bet you're jealous of my cotton-wear now, huh?"

Oh, hell yeah.

The park came up on the right before his imagination could take flight and he let out a disappointed breath. She still affected him the way she always had.

"Over there good?" She nodded toward a picnic table sitting under the shade of a giant willow tree.

"Perfect," he agreed, and kept pace with her as they wandered across the lot. "Haven't been here in a while. We used to skip lunch to throw a Frisbee around, then had to race back before class." Back when life seemed much simpler.

"I know," she said, sending him a sidelong glance. "I used to sit under this tree watching you—and your friends," she hurried to tack on. "None of you could keep a shirt on."

So, she'd noticed him as a scrawny junior—interesting. He'd known her, of course, as Jacob's little sister, but it was doubtful he could have picked her out of a group of girls back then. He'd been too focused on sports and having a good time with his friends to pay attention to a brunette with freckles across her nose. That came later.

He waited until she climbed the seat of the picnic table and sat on the top facing the water, then he removed his suit coat and unbuttoned the cuffs of his shirt, rolling them to his elbows. "There, that feels better." He glanced up to see her staring at his forearms as though mesmerized and hid a smile. "Nice day."

"Hmm?" she murmured, then jerked her gaze away. "Yes, I think we can safely say spring has arrived."

He hopped up to join her and leaned back on his arms, sighing in bliss as the sun bathed his face. "I miss this. My job requires me to spend the bulk of my days indoors, and no, I'm not trying to dissuade you from running in the election. In fact, I almost hope you win." Shocked by the truth in his statement, Trace sat up and met Mona's stare. "Well, there's a mic drop moment, if I ever heard one."

"You don't mean that, you can't. Sweetheart Cove

needs you." Mona grasped his hand and squeezed. "Between you and me—and that means keep quiet, for heaven's sake—I'm only in this thing to make a point, I definitely do *not* want to win."

He gazed at their hands and maneuvered so their fingers entwined. "I think you're stronger than you know, you'd make a great mayor."

"No, Trace. Get that thought out of your head. My hands are full at the restaurant. And now with Samantha getting ready to leave for college, I want to be able to fly out to see her when I get the chance, which wouldn't happen often enough if I was in your seat—so thanks, but no thanks." Mona broke their connection on the pretext of picking up her coffee. "Since it's unlikely the spa is going anywhere, as soon as council sees the necessity for better security and a larger dock to handle the extra tourists coming to the island, I plan to bow out of the race."

Trace picked up his own coffee and took a sip. "Commendable, but it doesn't work that way. If you want things done, you need to see them through."

"You think I don't know that?" she asked, her body tensing. "I'm a single mother who worked her ass off to give my girl the best I could. I don't need you telling *me* how to be a better person, Trace Michaels."

He raised his hands. "Whoa, you have to tell me how impressive you are—I already stand in awe. I've only been a single parent for a couple of years and already I'm drowning." He brushed a wayward strand of hair behind her ear, lingering for a moment before reluctantly letting go. "Why are you always on the defensive around me, Mona? I care about you, you must know that."

Tears stood out in her eyes, but she blinked them away and raised her chin. "Do you? Not enough to break up with me properly before I found you with Sally Hayward at our prom—the one you invited *me* to!"

He sat back, frowning. She was right. It didn't matter he'd had too much to drink and Sally had come on to him—he deserved Mona's wrath. Eighteen years, and yet it had obviously hurt her deep enough she still carried scars. Wounds he might never overcome.

"You know what, never mind." She jumped down and started toward her car. "This is a bad idea."

"Wait," Trace called, standing, but not following. His heart pounded with the fear that if he didn't get this right something rare and precious would be gone forever.

She slowed, then stopped, her back stiff and unyielding. "What do you want from me, Trace?"

Everything.

They'd been so in love once and those feelings were reawakening. He wanted a chance. "Don't leave.

We haven't even talked about Beth yet." Brilliant, Michaels, just brilliant.

Mona's shoulders dropped. "Not today. I need to go." She walked away, and this time he knew she wouldn't be back.

12

Beth sat on an overstuffed couch in the basement of her friend Lena's house and tried to look like she was enjoying herself. She didn't get invited to many parties and was actually good with that—it was tough being an introvert.

She cradled the beer someone had handed her and pretended to take a sip now and then, though it tasted pretty bad. The beat-up coffee table in front of her was filled with bottles and glasses, some lying on their side leaving little rivers of liquid to drip onto the floor. Some kids played spin the bottle a few feet away. She tried to hear what they were saying but the music was too loud, and she was too shy to get closer. And then Billy arrived and joined the circle. Beth's hands grew sweaty and the bottle slipped between her fingers, hitting the floor with a dull thunk. Her heart literally stopped, but thankfully the bass covered the noise.

"He's here," Lena shouted, leaning over the back of the couch.

"Shh!" Beth frowned up at her friend while sneaking embarrassed glances at Billy, who sat way-too-close to the annoying Sarah. "You're drunk."

Lena laughed like a hyena, tears rolling down her cheeks. "That's not all," she tittered, holding a finger and thumb together up to her lips. "Want some?"

Beth's first instinct was *hell, no*, but another glance to the nearby circle had her giving a hesitant nod. How bad could it be? Lena seemed fine, if goofy. She'd just have a little, enough to give her the courage to participate in the game.

Lena waved a guy over—a senior. He wrapped a tattooed arm around her waist and planted a wet kiss on her lips. Beth shuddered. He took a long drag on the thick joint, coughed up a lung, then passed it to Lena. She repeated the scenario and winked at Beth as she passed the dube over. Beth stared at it like it was a smoking gun. If her dad caught her, it could be.

A boy and a girl rose from the circle and stumbled over to a closet. They disappeared inside and the others erupted in cheers and catcalls. Sarah hugged Billy's arm and whispered something into his ear. The expression on his face twisted Beth's guts. Without another thought, she reached for the dope and took a long drag off the end. She was overcome by harsh coughs that made her eyes swim. Skunky-smelling smoke escaped her nose and mouth, burning tissue and lungs. After the haze cleared, her head felt foggy. The music pulsed through her body, filling her with false courage. Strength to do something she'd never do otherwise.

Ignoring the two making out behind her, she waited for her chance. The moment the closet door opened, she rose and staggered to the circle, picked up the green bottle, and said, "I dare Billy to go to the closet with me."

The group burst into laughter and someone snorted, "That's not how you play, dummy."

Beth swayed, dazed and confused. "Isn't this truth or dare? I dared."

"Yeah, but you need to spin the bottle to see who goes in there with you," The girl said helpfully.

Great. She'd risked the wrath of her father and it was all for nothing. And made an idiot out of herself—don't forget that happy addition. She started to slink away, wishing she could disappear into the beer-soaked floor when she heard two words that changed everything.

"I'll go."

Mona finished working on the restaurant's financial records and leaned back with a tired sigh. She kept promising herself she would hire a bookkeeper, but different calamities kept it from becoming a reality. In the last year, she'd had to replace the furnace, do costly repairs to the fire repression system, and update the cracked upholstery. The café did a steady business but hits like those definitely hurt the pocketbook. Oh well, maybe next year.

She shut down the computer and rose, intending to dive into a good book and a glass of red wine—not necessarily in that order—when Sam called her name, panic in her voice.

"Mom... Mom, Beth needs help. Can I borrow the car?" Footsteps thumped down the hall, matching Mona's increased heart rate. Sam skidded into the office, her face pale. "She's crying, Mom. I gotta go."

"Where is she?" *Why didn't she call her father?* Mona fumbled in her purse for the keys.

"Some party at a friend's house. She gave me the address." Sam clenched her hands. "She sounds really bad."

That sealed it. "I'm going with you." She swung the purse over her shoulder.

"What? No. She might take off. Is that what you want?" Samantha crossed her arms and shifted her torso forward, full of teenage angst.

Mona frowned. "Of course not, but I can't just sit by and wait, either. I'm going, or we call her dad—your choice."

"Fine, but let's hurry. I'm worried about her." Samantha dropped her arms and raced back the way she'd come.

Mona glanced at the desk phone, hesitated, then followed her daughter. Time enough to call Trace after she knew what they were dealing with—pray God, nothing serious.

The trip across town was made in tense silence with Mona sneaking sidelong glances at Samantha, who looked like a film noir star thanks to the flickering streetlamps lighting up the vehicle on the moonless night.

"Beth's a smart girl, honey. I'm sure she'll be fine," Mona murmured, while waiting for a traffic light to change to green.

Sam shrugged and huddled down in her corner. "I hope you're right. She sounded... strange."

Strange? What did that mean? The light changed and she punched the gas, suddenly filled with dread. There was so much that could happen to a teenage girl. Thank goodness, Samantha was level-headed. And then she felt immediately guilty for thinking that thought. Bad things happened to anyone at any time, without rhyme or reason—fate really could be a bitch.

They pulled up in front of a modest two-story house in a residential cul-de-sac. The upper floor was dark and quiet, but light and sound poured out of the downstairs windows, opened to the night. Mona was surprised the neighbors hadn't already called the police. Cars lined the street, and a couple had even pulled up on the party spot's lawn. Someone's parents weren't going to be impressed come morning.

"Do you see her?" she asked, peering through the windshield.

"No," Sam said, leaning out of her open window. "I'm going to run in and see if I can find her."

Mona's first reaction was, *over my dead body*, but she realized there wasn't much choice. If she went in, the kids would scramble, making it almost impossible to get Beth out safely. But she didn't have to like it.

"Ten minutes and then I'm calling the cops. Beth's a minor, what was she thinking?"

"Probably that she wanted to have fun, Mom. Didn't you ever make a mistake as a kid?" Sam stared at her with all the worldly wisdom of a young woman. "I'll be right back." She climbed out of the car, then leaned on the windowsill. "Thanks for coming, love you."

Love you, too. Mona stared after her with blurry eyes. She'd been blessed ever since the day the doctor laid a crying, pink bundle of joy on her chest. No matter what, she'd never regretted giving birth to Trace's baby—their daughter.

She swiped at her wet cheeks just as Sam reappeared with her arm wrapped around Beth's hunched form. Mona hurried to help, frowning at the stench of booze and... weed? that permeated her clothes. The girl's quiet sobs ripped at her heart. She put away her misgivings to offer the support she so clearly needed.

"Hush, honey, we've got you now." She added her arm to Samantha's, and between them they managed to get her down the driveway and into the backseat of the car.

Sam climbed in after her and looked up at Mona. "I'll ride with her. She shouldn't be alone right now."

Mona nodded. She'd seen the torn shirt and mussed hair. She shuddered to imagine what that might mean. Trace needed to know; they could no longer put off contacting him.

She cast an angry glare at the house, then circled the car, climbed in, and hurried to start the engine. A moment later warm air circulated through the interior. Before drawing away, she turned, looked at the girls, and asked the toughest question she'd ever had to voice. "Beth, I know this is hard, but honey, were you assaulted?"

"Mom!" Samantha gazed at her with wide eyes. "What a thing to say."

Mona's stomach was twisted into a labyrinth of knots, but she needed an answer. "If she was, she needs to go to the hospital. They can check her over and make sure she's not injured." She couldn't say rape, it was too brutal.

"Can I just go to your house, please?" Beth whispered, her face pale and drawn under the streetlamp. "I'm fine. I just... fell."

Mona hesitated, torn between having her properly looked at and understanding how scared she must feel. "Okay, but we're going to call your father when we get there—no arguments. He deserves to know what happened."

Beth shuddered and drew a deep breath. "Yes, ma'am." Then she turned her head into Sam's shoulder and cried like her heart was breaking. Mona sympathized. She felt the same way.

13

After an emotionally taxing Friday, Trace was ready for a beer. Beth was staying over at a friend's, so he called Jacob to meet him at the Blue Cup, a new bar near the wharf.

By the time he'd gone home to shower and change, the parking lot was packed. He parked down the block and tapped the steering wheel, debating whether he wanted the hassle of pushing himself into a noisy pub just to get a drink. He had beer at home, and it would be a hell of a lot quieter. *Lonelier too.*

One drink wasn't going to hurt him. If he wasn't careful, he'd start going to bed by nine and walking outside in his robe to grab the newspaper. He wasn't an old man, though there were days he felt like one. Maybe he'd even hook up with someone, go out on a date. Between the divorce and raising his daughter, he'd placed his own needs on the back burner, but lately his libido was making itself known and it was all Mona's fault. It was strange to think they lived in the same town, had once been intimate, and her brother was Trace's best friend, yet it was their daughters' friendship that had brought them together. Well, not together, together, though he wished for... more.

At least it was a nice night. If he had too much to drink, walking home wouldn't be a hardship. Spring in the Pacific Northwest was notorious for rain and variable temperatures, but he wouldn't need his umbrella tonight.

The music got louder, the closer he drew to the propped open entrance door. People spilled onto the sidewalk like ants, milling around in groups of three or four, laughing and talking and passing around cigarettes—at least he hoped they were cigarettes.

"Hey, Trace, socializing with the riff-raff?"

Trace squinted to see the owner of the familiar voice. "Liz, is that you?"

The tall blonde separated herself from the throng and waved. "It's been a long week, time to unwind."

Amen to that. Trace nodded. "I'm sorry about the burglary, Liz. I hadn't heard until the other day. Did they catch the culprit?"

"Not yet." She sighed. "I'm not holding out much hope. Mona Samuels is working on organizing a community crime watch. We're having a meeting next week. Maybe it will help."

He should have thought of that. It was his job as mayor to coordinate with law enforcement to solve criminal concerns. "I'm glad Mona has a handle on the issue. Please let me know if there's anything I can do. I heard the damage to your flower shop was quite extensive."

"Yes. Thank goodness for insurance though, right?" She smiled and embraced his arm. "Buy me a drink?"

The warm weight of her breast pressing into his arm should have spiked his interest, but for some reason he only felt uncomfortable. What was the matter with him?

"Sure," he said, unwinding from her grasp on the pretext of holding the door for her to enter the dark bar. Mood lights were spaced out along the walls in between giant speakers blaring music from the band performing on a narrow stage at the far end of the room. Couples gyrated on the floor in a facsimile of the dance moves he'd learned in grade school. Tables and booths filled to overflowing took up the rest of the space with a long bar that ran the length of the back wall.

He looked around, but it was almost impossible to pick Jacob out of this crowd. He'd send his buddy a text after a quick cocktail with Liz. He nodded toward a table newly vacated and she smiled her agreement. A server met them as they arrived and efficiently cleared glasses and wiped the tabletop down all while holding a tray full of heavy looking bottles and drinks at shoulder height with her other hand.

"What can I get you?" she asked, making room on the tray for the dirties.

"I'll take a beer, whatever's on tap," Trace said, admiring her balancing skills. "What about you, Liz?"

"Same thing, thanks." She smiled at the woman, then turned her attention to the band. "They're good," she yelled, tapping her toes to the beat. She slid Trace a flirty glance. "Do you dance?"

"Not well," he lied. "Go ahead though, I don't mind."

She laughed. "You aren't getting rid of me that fast. So tell me, Trace Michaels, what brings you out on a Friday night?"

Good question. One he didn't have an answer for anymore. This wasn't his scene. He preferred quiet background music and a romantic setting for a date—not that this was one. Liz seemed like a nice woman, and maybe if he wasn't hooked on Mona...

"Oh, oh. I know that look," she murmured. "You're already taken, aren't you? Who's the lucky lady?"

He shrugged uncomfortably. "It's not like that. We're just friends."

"Ah, ha, that's what they all say, honey. You better tell her how you feel before it's too late." She paused and tipped her head. "Is she a local girl?"

He reluctantly nodded. Liz deserved that much from him. "We used to go out—a long time ago."

"You did? Wait. Wait, is it... *Mona*?" Her voice climbed a couple of octaves, her lips curving into a pleased smirk.

Trace scrunched his shoulders and glanced around to make sure no one was listened. "Shh, I don't need it to be a public announcement," he muttered.

"Sorry, but after the hell that ex-wife gave you and the rumors she's spreading, you deserve a little happiness." Liz took a sip of the foamy beer the server dropped off on her way to the next table and nodded her satisfaction. "This is good, try it."

He ignored her request, focused instead on her previous words. "What rumor? I haven't heard anything."

She swept her hair over her shoulder and gave him a look. "Not surprising. You're kind of busy running our town, aren't you?" She frowned. "Maybe I shouldn't have said anything. You know how these things are, it'll blow over."

Trace reached for her hand, cool from cradling the frosted glass mug. "Tell me, Liz."

She stared at him, then pulled her hand away,

folding it into her lap. "Fine, but don't say I didn't warn you." She glanced around, then leaned over the table and lowered her voice. "Rumor is Samantha is your daughter, Trace."

ONCE THEY ARRIVED HOME, Mona made sure Beth wasn't physically injured before sending her off for a warm bath while she made tea with honey and set out a plate of banana bread and oatmeal cookies. Sometimes, comfort food helped where words couldn't.

"I'm worried about her, Mom." Sam leaned against the kitchen counter and watched the kettle heating on the stove, her gaze pensive.

Mona stopped her needless fidgeting with the dessert plate to embrace her daughter. "I know, me too. But she'll be okay. We'll take good care of her now." She closed her eyes and inhaled the Organza perfume Samantha had taken to wearing and thanked the Almighty for keeping the girls safe. Beth could have been seriously hurt tonight. As it was, the psychological effects of what she'd been through would probably weigh on her for a long time to come. They would have to talk later, after she calmed down and her father was here.

Trace. He was bound to flip a gasket when he

found out. The more she thought about it, the more Mona became convinced she should tell him face-to-face. It wasn't the sort of news she wanted to impart over the phone.

The kettle whistled and she released Samantha to turn off the heat and pour the boiling water into the porcelain teapot she'd found at a yard sale one summer. "Tea's ready. I'm going to check on Beth and then leave you girls to it while I drive over to her dad's house to deliver the news. Will you be okay until I get back?"

"Sure. Maybe we'll watch a movie, or something." Sam picked at the edge of a cookie. "Mom? Thanks for helping tonight. I wouldn't have handled it so well on my own."

Mona's throat grew tight. "I think you might have surprised yourself, but I'm glad I was there. I love you, you know."

She grinned. "Me too."

"Brat." Mona laughed and headed upstairs, the smile fading the closer she came to the bathroom door. She stared at it for a few seconds before knocking—trying, without success, to come up with words to heal some of the pain that poor child was going through. In the end, she decided to stay pragmatic.

"Tea and cookies in the kitchen. You have five minutes, missy."

"Okay," Beth called, her voice only slightly wobbly.

Mona pressed a hand to the wood. She remembered the emotional turmoil of her own teenage years and knew time was the best remedy.

She returned downstairs, grabbed her keys from where she'd left them, and stepped outside. Stars peeked between the clouds like a beacon of hope and her traitorous heart raced at the prospect of seeing Trace.

She made the drive to his house in a quiet panic. Now that the time was near, she didn't know how to break the news. Whatever she said, he'd be furious. Somehow, she had to convince him to calm down and think before doing anything he might regret. Beth needed him.

The windows were dark, and his car was missing from the driveway. She hadn't considered he might be out. Just because she had no life, didn't mean everyone spent their Friday nights at home eating popcorn and watching old movies. What if he was on a date? She didn't want to get caught sitting in front of his home like a peeping Susie, awkward wouldn't begin to cover that scenario. Yet, she needed to talk to him. She pulled the cellphone from the rear pocket of her jeans, her finger hovering over the keypad as she stared at his home. Maybe Jacob knew something. She dialed his number and waited impatiently for her brother to pick up.

"Yeah," he shouted into the speaker, making her jump. Music blasted the cab of her car, along with the sound of pool balls clacking together and people laughing. A bar? Jacob wasn't really the bar type—especially after losing his wife to a drunk driver.

"Jake? Where are you?" She found herself shouting back and cringed, imagining the phone up to his ear.

"The Blue Cup," he answered in a more normal tone, the sound muting as he moved away from the crowd. "I was supposed to meet Trace here for a beer, but this place is a madhouse tonight. I haven't found him yet."

"Are you sure he didn't stand you up?" She set the phone in its cradle and started her car.

"He's here, or at least his vehicle is. What do you need?" His voice was clear now. He must have gone outside.

"I need to talk to Trace. Beth got into a bit of trouble tonight." Mona pulled out and headed downtown. She hadn't been to the new pub yet, but heard it was a popular hangout for the millennial crowd. Liz had invited her to a girls' night out a couple of times, but she'd put it off. Maybe she should go. It sounded as though Trace got out often enough. She ignored the hot flare in her chest to make the turn onto Wharf Street. Even from a distance she could see where the bar was by the cars parked along the street.

"I'm just pulling up, wait for me."

"Yeah, sure, but then I'm heading home. I don't like to leave Josie and Jane alone for too long," Jacob warned before clicking off.

If only she could meet someone like her brother, Mona reflected as she searched for a place to park. He was one in a million.

A little red sports car pulled out, and with a bit of maneuvering she managed to wrangle her beast into the stall. She shut off the engine and opened her door, then hesitated, pulling down the visor to check out her face in the compact mirror. Well, she wasn't about to win any beauty contests, that's for sure. She pinched her cheeks for color and bit her lips lightly, then sighed and climbed out of the car. She wasn't here to go on a manhunt anyway.

Jacob paced the sidewalk near the front entry and looked up as she approached. "Is Beth hurt?"

Trust her brother to zero in on the important stuff. "No, just shook up. I'll tell you about it tomorrow, after I talk to Trace. Any chance you could do a walk-through with me?"

He nodded. "I wouldn't let you go in there alone. What do you take me for?" He turned and led the way, his wide shoulders bulldozing a path through the congested entry. "We'll stick together," he said over his shoulder as the noise hit them in the face. "It's safer that way."

She smiled her gratitude and stuck close to his back as they navigated the room, looking for a familiar blond head. They were almost to the bar when she saw him leaning over a two-seater table talking intently to a woman—Liz.

She stumbled to a halt while Jacob forged ahead, clapping a hand on his friend's shoulder to break up the *tête-à-tête*. Trace looked annoyed until he realized who it was, then he smiled and rose to clasp Jacob's hand. When he turned to introduce his date, he noticed Mona and froze. Funny, she couldn't move either.

He looked good—great, really in a pair of dockers and a button-down shirt in powder blue. She'd expected him to be somewhat embarrassed, considering their past, but she didn't expect the raw anger blazing out of his eyes.

Liz turned to see who he was staring at and a guilty expression chased across her face before she, too, rose and hurried to greet her. "Mona, I wasn't expecting to see you here. This isn't what it looks like," she added in a near-whisper.

Mona forced a shrug though she felt like a glass that might shatter at any moment. "He's a free man. He can go out with whoever he wants."

"There's something I need to tell you," she said urgently, then went quiet as Trace came up behind her.

"Outside. Now." He took her arm and forcibly turned her toward the door.

"Hey, what the hell, man?" Jacob yelled after them.

"Stay out of my way," Trace ordered. "Your sister and I have some... catching up to do."

The way he said it made Mona's blood run cold.

He knew.

That was the only possible explanation. She didn't know how he'd found out, but Trace knew he was Samantha's father. She'd dreaded this day for eighteen years and now that it was here a strange sort of calm—almost relief—came over her. No more hiding from the truth. She only hoped when the dust settled, she'd be able to pick up the pieces of her tattered life.

14

The betrayal cut deep. Trace had a hard time controlling the urge to shake Mona until the truth came out of her lying lips. All these years... It didn't even bear thinking about. She'd taken his daughter away from him. How could she do that to him? To Samantha?

"Trace, please. I can explain." Mona tugged ineffectively against the grip he had on her arm. "You're hurting me."

He stopped walking so fast she plowed into his back. He turned on her, rage taking over like a hungry beast. "That's rich coming from you. She's seventeen fricking years old. Were you *ever* going to tell me?"

She flinched, the guilt in her eyes turning his stomach.

"You weren't, were you?" He shook his head, a

harsh laugh scratching his throat raw. "Well, at least I know where I stand with you."

"People are looking. Can you quit shouting, please?" She made another effort to get free, and he yanked her up against his chest.

"Do you think I give a *shit* what anyone thinks?" He glanced around and realized she was right, they were creating a scene. He turned back to her, staring at the woman he'd thought different from the others—someone he could see in his life. She looked as miserable as he felt.

He opened his hands and let her go. "Let's get out of here."

"I... I need to—" Mona rubbed her arm where he'd held her and shivered. "Wh... where do you want to go?"

He was still mad as hell, but guilt roiled around in his gut, too. He'd never hurt a woman before. It didn't make him proud for doing it now. If only she'd told him the truth. What did she think he would have done, fought for custody? They'd been kids. He certainly hadn't been in a place to raise a daughter—not then anyway. He'd deserved the right to know, though. And he deserved an explanation now.

"My place. Unless you're scared?" he taunted. She aught to be.

Not his Mona. No, she raised her chin and led the

way toward the parked cars. "I'm frightened of letting the ghosts of the past out," she said. "But, I'm not afraid of you."

Wish he could say the same. She terrified him. He should hate her for the deception, but now that he was calming down, he could maybe see why she'd done it. *Not* that it excused the lie, just that it made it easier to bear somehow.

"We'll take my car." He pointed toward his SUV. "I'll bring you back later for yours." She hesitated, then moved to stand by the passenger door, waiting for him to click the locks. He opened the door for her, aware of the soft rustle of her jeans as she climbed into the cab, then strode around the back to give himself a moment's privacy to get his head on straight. This wasn't a date, dammit, and she wasn't the woman of his dreams. Reality had blown that fantasy apart. He'd have to see where they went from here.

She was shivering harder when he got into the car, so he turned up the heat as soon as he started the engine and reached in the back for his jacket. "Here. Wrap up in this before you catch a cold." She was wearing one of those thin blouse things women liked so much that did nothing toward protecting the core.

"Thanks," she whispered, gazing sideways at him with big eyes. "Why are you being nice to me?"

Good question. Because he didn't like being a dick.

He'd never found it accomplished much other than bad feelings.

He leaned one arm over the steering wheel and turned to face her. She looked like a kid, wrapped up in his jacket like that. Something warm moved through his chest. Okay, so the attraction hadn't died. Instead, of bringing joy, it just made him sad. He could never trust her again, and without trust they had nothing.

He reached out and brushed her hair behind her ear. "I could have fallen hard for you," he murmured.

She flinched and pulled away, her eyes tearing up. "I guess that means it's too late for us, then?"

Annoyed with the entire situation, he slammed his palm on the steering wheel. "What do you expect? I can't just hide this under the carpet and go on about my life, Mona. I want my daughter to know who I am." A sudden horrible thought came to him. "She doesn't know, does she?"

Mona's eyes gleamed in the dark cab. "Of course not. Do you seriously think she would have kept quiet all these years if she did?"

He sat back and stared out the windshield. "Why not? You did."

"I guess I deserve that." She sighed. "Have you ever built a snowman? You start with a small, perfect ball, then you roll it and roll it until it turns into this amazing thing you've created with your very own hands. But sometimes, the little ball gets away from you. It careens down a hill, gathering momentum, until it smashes into a thousand pieces and there's no way to put it back together again." She sat up and turned to him. "That's what happened to us, Trace. We had something special, didn't we?"

He couldn't deny it, he'd fallen hard for Mona. They'd spent hours together, talking and laughing and loving. Until he destroyed her trust. Guess turnabout was fair play.

"Yes," he admitted. "And I'm sorry for my part in smashing our relationship on the rocks, as per your awful analogy." He smiled. "But that didn't give you the right to keep my daughter away from me. From Beth. My daughter has a sister," he said with a touch of wonder. As the certainty settled in his gut, his mind jumped to the future. Sam was going to college soon, it was all Beth could talk about. He needed to find a way for the three of them to spend time as a family before she was out of their lives again–though only temporarily. He wasn't letting this opportunity slip through his fingers.

"I'm scared," Mona whispered. "What if Sam hates me after I tell her the truth?"

His instinct was to wrap her in his arms and assure her they would work it out together, but instead he clenched the steering wheel and stared outside as an inebriated group stumbled down the street to a waiting taxi. He half-wished he was drunk. He could use a buffer for his topsy-turvy heart about now.

"Did Jacob know?" he suddenly asked. The man was his best friend. If he'd hidden...

"No! I told you, no one knew. I didn't even fill out the father's name on her birth certificate," Mona cried, then clasped a hand to her mouth. "Oh, Trace, I'm sorry."

He glared at her. "So you were too ashamed to even put me down on a court document? That's just great."

She held her hand out, fingers trembling. "It wasn't like that. I was young and scared. Af... after we broke up, it was the darkest time in my life. And then I found out I was pregnant. You were already engaged to that, that woman—I couldn't tell you. Maybe, I wanted to hurt you, though you didn't even know about the baby. My parents pressured me, and Jacob (your friend) swore he'd beat the crap out of whoever did that to me —don't you see, I didn't have a choice." Tears rolled silently down her cheeks.

He cursed Sally all over again. "Here's the funny part. I only asked her to marry me because she said she was pregnant." Mona gasped, her eyes going wide. "I didn't find out until much later it was a lie. There was no baby. She didn't like that I chose you instead of her, so she decided to break us up. And I let it happen. I take full responsibility for allowing that to happen. By the time I found out, Bethany was born. I couldn't walk away from her. Turned out I didn't have to." He let his head fall against the headrest and closed his eyes. So many wasted years.

"What a mess," she said.

They both sat silently for a while, the heater lulling them into a tentative peace. The stars were out on full display, twinkling diamonds in a velvet sky. The traffic had died down and the waves lapping against the quay seemed to beat a message of forgiveness into his heart. It was done. Neither one could change the past, but they could make a difference to their future. He just had to take the first step.

He lifted his head and looked at her. Maybe she wasn't perfect, but then, neither was he. They had done something right though; they'd created a daughter together. It mattered. Mona mattered.

"Look—" he started.

"Oh, no," Mona cried, sitting up and clutching his arm. "With everything else that happened, I forgot to tell you why I was looking for you."

She'd been searching for him? Her face had gone pale again, and he'd have bruises from where she'd pinched his arm. His pulse kicked, a sick feeling invading his gut. "What is it? What happened?"

"She's fine. Just shook up. I made sure he didn't... She was in the bath and I thought I should tell you face-to-face, but then the other stuff happened, and..."

The words buzzed in his head. Shook up. Bath. Beth. Something had happened to his baby girl.

He shook her off and ground the gearshift into reverse. "Where is she?" he roared. The car exploded out of the parking spot and accelerated down the road, mirroring his mood.

"M... My house. Sam is with her." Mona scrambled to put her seatbelt on and huddled against her side of the car.

Good thing, because at the moment, murder was starting to seem pretty damn tempting.

15

Even though Sam's mom wanted her to join them downstairs, Beth stayed in the bathtub until her skin resembled a prune. As the water cooled, she used her toe to add more hot, though nothing seemed to rid her of the full-body shivers she'd endured since leaving Lena's house. She was being silly, she knew that. Nothing even really happened. It's just... it could have. Thank goodness her dad had insisted on Judo lessons when she was younger. She smirked, recalling Billy's stunned look as he lay crumpled on the floor, hands cupping his groin.

The worst part came when she pulled her shirt together and opened the door to a crowd of shocked faces. Instead of the support Beth had expected, she received taunts and criticism of her childish reaction.

"What did you invite him in there for, if it wasn't to

make out? You're such a baby," the blonde who'd been cuddled up to him earlier scoffed, as she and the rest of the circle brushed past to help the fallen anti-hero.

Stunned at the vicious words and shocked by Billy's attack—because, that's what it had essentially been—Beth stumbled past the rest of the partygoers, head down, intent on getting far away. She flinched when Lena moved out of a guy's arms and grabbed the front of her shirt.

"Whooee, looks like you had a good time." She wobbled from side to side, her eyes glassy. "Come back whenever you want. We always have fun, don't we?" She smiled up at the guy who'd wrapped his arms around her waist and was nuzzling her neck while watching Beth with predatory eyes.

"Yeah," he agreed with a wolf's smile. "We'll keep you... occupied."

Seriously freaked out, Beth unhooked the claws holding her shirt, and lurched for the stairs, positive she could feel their hot breath chasing her up the steps. The moment she escaped the foul odors and rapacious crowd, she ducked into the trees lining the drive and collapsed on the ground, sobbing. Finally, she pulled herself together enough to call Sam for help. There was no way she wanted her dad to see her like this—he'd ground her for life.

Mona had been so nice, not judgmental at all.

She'd simply bundled Samantha and Beth into the car and taken them home to this bath, and tea waiting downstairs. Sam's mom was the best. At least she cared about her kid, not like Beth's own mother.

The water had grown cold again, it was time to face the music. She climbed out and dressed in the cozy pajamas Sam found for her, smiling at the pizza and unicorn images on a powder blue background.

The house was quiet, and she had to subdue the urge to tiptoe down the stairs. She was safe now even if her poor heart hadn't caught up to the program yet. That was the last party she planned on attending —*ever*.

"Sam?" she called, glancing up and down the short hallway.

"In the kitchen," her friend replied.

Beth clasped the material within the too-long sleeves and entered the room, opening her mouth to tease Sam about her taste in sleepwear. Except she wasn't alone. Mona sat at the oversized kitchen table, a steaming cup clasped between her hands and a worried frown marring her normally cheerful face, and across from her—Beth's dad.

He rose as soon as she appeared, his eyes dark and inscrutable. "I thought you were staying at a friend's house?"

She shot Sam a panicked glance and tried to take

heart from her encouraging look. "Lena invited me over, but I didn't know she was having a party, Daddy." Her hands were sweaty, and she refused to meet his gaze, sure guilt was stamped on her forehead.

"Well," he said, coming to stand in front of her, "that's funny. When I called her, she didn't know anything about a sleepover, just that you were '*stoked*', her word, for her big spring break party."

Yup, grounded for life. She lifted her eyes to his face and the compassion and love she saw there made her chest hurt. "I'm sorry, Dad. I never should have lied."

He cupped her cheeks and kissed her brow. "No, you shouldn't have, and we *will* be talking about that, but right now I need to know my baby girl is all right—are you?"

So many times in the past, her father had been there when she tripped and fell. He was her rock, but this was something she had to handle on her own. Guess that meant she was growing up—and she'd thought being a kid was tough.

"I'm going to be, now that you're here." She turned to Mona. "Thanks for coming to get me, and for breaking the news to my dad. It means a lot."

Mona's smile trembled on her lips. "You're welcome, honey, anytime." Her gaze went to Beth's dad with sad acceptance. "Can you girls sit down for a minute, please? We have something to tell you."

Samantha moved to her mom's side. "What's wrong, Mom? You look upset."

Mona took her hand and kissed the palm, tears leaking from the corners of her eyes. "Not upset, honey, just... overwhelmed, I guess."

Concerned, Beth searched her dad's face, but for once, his expression was stoic. "Sit down. This is going to be a bit of a shock," he warned.

She took a chair across from Samantha, her stomach in knots over the palpable tension in the room. "It'll be okay," Beth whispered, reaching out to grasp her hand in comfort. *Please don't let it be cancer or some other horrible news.*

Sam's smile trembled. "I hope you're right."

Mona started to rise. "How about some tea? I could use..."

"After," Beth's dad said, crossing and then uncrossing his arms. "Let's get this over with."

Mona's jaw clenched, but she resumed her seat. "Fine. Would you like to start?" Her eyes shot sparks, and Sam's overly warm hand squeezed Beth's.

"Samantha, I don't know if you're aware of this, but your mother and I dated back in high school." Beth's dad said, his gaze ping-ponging between the three women.

Sam nodded and swallowed hard. "I... I know," she said, half under her breath.

Mona leaned forward. "How did you find out?" she asked. "It was a long time ago."

Sam turned to her mom. "People talk, Mom. It's hard to keep anything secret these days." She let go of Beth's fingers and placed her hands in her lap. "It's no big deal, right?"

Beth's brows scrunched together. It almost sounded as though Samantha didn't want to hear about their parents' old love affair. She thought it was kind of cool. No wonder she'd felt an immediate connection to the Samuels family.

Obviously, Mona picked up on her daughter's reluctance as well. "What *else* did you hear, Sam?"

Surprising Beth, her dad moved around the table and crouched by Sam's side, his arm resting on the table. "Whatever it is, we'll work it out together. Okay, sweetheart?"

Samantha looked at him and nodded, her lips trembling. "Are you my dad?" she asked.

Mona gasped, her heart threatening to take wing right out of her chest. "How long have you known?" she whispered, tears thick in her throat.

Sam's blue eyes—so like her father's—widened. "It's true then?" She pushed her chair back, almost knocking Trace over, and rose to confront them. "All these years and you kept it from me?" She glanced across the table. "From Beth? What the hell?"

"Samantha, don't talk to your mother that way." Trace reprimanded, rising to face her. "There were... reasons she kept quiet about me. What matters is that she's telling you, us, now."

"Please, baby," Mona begged, her face drawn. "I would never do anything to purposely hurt you."

"Wouldn't you, Mom? Really?" Sam brushed away tears with angry swipes that threatened to take the skin from her cheeks. "Do you know how tough it was to go to a father/daughter dance with Uncle Jacob when everyone else was there with their dads? And what about baseball camp, huh, Mom? I couldn't go because you had the damn restaurant and U... Uncle Jacob had a new baby." She was openly sobbing now, her eyes red and nose blotchy. "And all the time he's been right here!"

Mona tried to take Samantha in her arms, but she was too worked up. Instead of protecting her daughter, she'd broken her heart—and her own in the process.

"You need to calm down so we can talk this through," Trace said, attempting to pat her back.

"Leave me alone," she cried, dropping to her knees and covering her face with her hands.

"Quit fighting," Beth yelled, toppling her chair as she pushed away from the table. "It doesn't matter, don't you see? We aren't alone anymore." She knelt beside Sam and wrapped an arm around her shaking back. "We aren't alone. You have a dad now, and I have a mom, and we have each other. *Sisters*." She rested her cheek on Sam's shoulder. "We're sisters, Sam."

Mona covered her mouth to hold back the hiccupping cries as Samantha slowly raised her head and looked from one to the other of them before finally coming to rest on Beth.

"How did you get so smart?" she asked, returning her embrace.

"I have a pretty great family," Beth answered, her smile wiping away the ugliness of the past few moments.

Mona's gaze went to Trace and the next moment they were huddled over their girls in the most wonderful hug of all.

She knew there would be questions and a learning curve in their future, but for once, she wasn't afraid. Whether she and Trace sorted out their past and gave the future a try or not, they had each other's back and that was a pretty damn good feeling.

EPILOGUE

One Month Later,

Mona tightened her grip on Trace's arm. "This better be worth it, Mister. I'm getting vertigo." He'd placed the blindfold over her eyes before they'd started out on their journey. They'd driven for a ways, laughing and talking, then he'd helped her from his car and led her down this unknown trail. She had a feeling they were near water, she could hear the squawk of gulls and smell the fresh, briny scent of the ocean.

"It's not far. Now be patient," he promised.

A playful breeze teased her hair and slid beneath her blouse, lifting it to dance around her body. "What's with all the secrecy, anyway?"

The past few weeks had been a whirlwind, what with her resigning from the mayoral race—with the council and Trace's promise to look into her concerns—

and planning family excursions so Sam could get to know her father. Every steppingstone in their relationship was a blessing for Mona. Her greatest fear had been realized—Trace knew about her deception—and surprisingly enough, the sky hadn't fallen. If anything, once the shock was over, they were learning to fit into each other's lives better than she could ever have expected.

He stopped and grasped her arm with his other hand. "We're here. Are you ready?" He moved to stand in front of her, and as he lifted the blindfold from her eyes, he leaned in and brushed her lips in a tender kiss. "Welcome home, sweetheart."

Lost in the feel of his mouth on hers, it took a moment for Mona to process what he'd said. She opened her eyes, smiling into his beloved face, then glanced around, her gaze widening in surprise. "You brought me to Sunset Beach? I thought you said you never come out here?"

He nodded and led her to a blanket laid out on the sand with a picnic basket, wine and two glasses, set nearby. "That's true, but I plan on changing that in the future." He kissed her again, their lips melding together—two halves of a whole. "Look in the basket, honey."

Heart thumping madly, Mona met his encouraging look, then slowly opened the wicker lid. She tried not to be disappointed by the sheaf of papers bundled within, but for a moment there...

"What is this?" she asked, drawing the stack out. She glanced through them, but her eyes weren't tracking, and she soon gave up to look at Trace. "It seems to be a sales agreement, is it?"

His mouth quirked. "Good deduction, Watson. I should have remembered how impatient you can be." He took the papers and set them aside to draw her into his arms. "How do you feel about a house with a waterfront view to rival your brother's?"

She stared at him as the implications began to set in. "Did you buy this land?" She gazed around them at the gently swelling surf, the long stretch of sandy beach, the privacy. "Oh, my God, you did. You bought Sunset Beach."

"Well, technically we did," he murmured. "That's what I was trying to show you. We own equal shares, Mona. This is your land as much as it is mine."

Stunned, she could only stare at him, trying to take in what he'd done for her. She'd always dreamed of having her own land, a place where she could leave her mark for future generations, and now... "I don't know what to say," she whispered.

His smile faded, replaced by intensity. "There's something else in the basket, take a look."

Her hands shook so badly she could barely draw

out the blue velvet box nestled in the bottom of the hamper. She turned to Trace, holding it in her palm like it was a precious treasure, only to see him bowed before her on one knee.

"I know this is probably too soon, but when it's right, it's right. I've never met anyone like you, Mona. You're kind, generous, a wonderful mother, and so beautiful you take my breath away. I love you, sweetheart. Will you please, please do me the honor of becoming my bride? "

Tears fell and she blinked them away, not wanting to miss a second of this dream, because that's what it felt like. How did she get so lucky?

With a little yelp of joy, she threw herself into his arms and they both fell onto the blanket laughing. "Yes, yes, a million times yes," she cried, kissing every square inch of his face. When their lips met, she sighed. Home indeed.

AFTERWORD

Reviews are the lifeblood of any successful author. Without you, we can't be heard.

If you enjoy the story, please consider sharing on your favorite social media sites, as well as GoodReads and from wherever you've bought the book.

Thank you,

Jacquie Biggar

Jacqbiggar.com

FREE DOWNLOAD

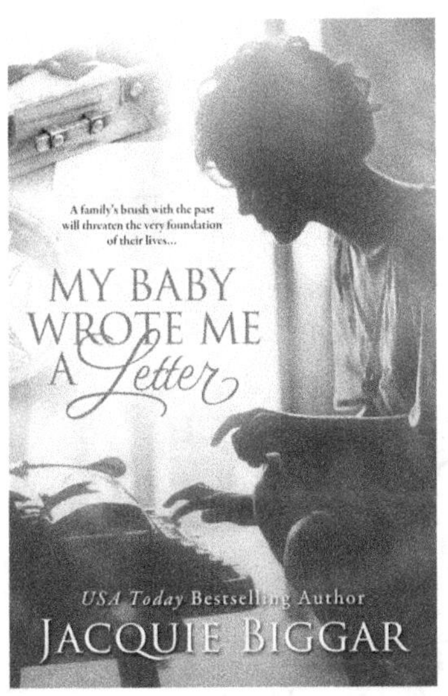

My Baby Wrote Me A Letter

A family's brush with the past will threaten the fabric of their lives.

Eight months pregnant and her Navy husband away on a mission, Grace Freeman craves the security of her childhood home in Canada.

When a letter written by her long-lost mother is found in an old writing desk it creates a tear in the fabric of her family.

Can Grace find a way to bring peace to those she loves, or will a message from the past destroy their future?

Newsletter subscribers also get bonus content and insider information every month. I love giveaways and there is lots of interesting stuff for me to share with you!

Newsletter- Sign up Now!

PREVIEW THE SISTER PACT

Chapter One

Holly Tremaine glared after the cabbie who'd just driven away with her carefully wrapped Christmas gifts in the backseat. She'd done everything short of flying to catch his attention, all to no avail. Now what was she going to do? She hadn't even caught the number of his taxi. The car was blue and white, and the cab driver had been an older man with pictures of his two grandchildren taped to his dash—that's all the information she had.

What a mess.

The bluebird of lost hopes—aka the cab—disappeared into the busy Victoria traffic leaving Holly alone to face her past. She swallowed hard and turned toward her parents' imposing two-story townhouse. The dismal day blended with the gray stone and black iron accents that had intimidated her as a child—nice to see some things remained the same.

Sighing, she tightened her grip on the carry-on bag she'd limited herself to for the flight—which is why she was now giftless—and trudged toward the big oak doors as though she were fighting her way through quicksand. Great. Not even in the house and she already regretted the trip.

The sign below the bell was no less glaring for the elegant script; No Soliciting, Fundraising, Salesmen, Religion or Politics- Thank you.

As though attaching manners at the end softened

the cold tone the message conveyed. That was her parents in a nutshell.

She jabbed the bell like it was a release valve for her frustration. The rain that had held off while she dashed from store to store began to fall—a misty drizzle that sank into Holly's clothes and turned her hair lank in a matter of seconds. Wet and miserable, she waited for someone to let her in.

The door swung back revealing a yawning black maw—or so it seemed in that moment. The one person Holly had hoped to avoid stood in the entry.

Her sister.

"Holly." Susan looked down her slender, too perfect, nose. "You're late."

Holly blew a wayward strand of wet hair away from her face and tried to ignore the tic developing over her right eyebrow. "Well, I'm here now. Better late than never, right?" She glanced over her shoulder at the curtain of rain. "Mind letting me in? It's cold out here." She smiled and took a step forward, forcing her sister to move or get plowed down.

The grand entrance was just as inhospitable as she remembered. Dark wood climbed the walls while marble tile covered the floor like a layer of ice. Eight years and nothing had changed.

"Where are they?" she asked, though she knew the

answer by glancing at her watch. Five o'clock, time for pre-dinner drinks in the lounge.

"Mom and Dad? Or Steven?"

The nervous tap-tapping of Susan's glossy black pump told Holly she wasn't nearly as calm as she pretended. For her part, Holly couldn't control the fluttering in her stomach at the thought of seeing Steven after all these years. Her sister looked... older—harder. Maybe married life hadn't turned out like she expected. Was it wrong Holly hoped that was true?

"I just arrived, Sue." They'd both used nicknames for each other as children. "Can we save the arguing until tomorrow? I'm beat."

Susan's expression softened as though she, too, regretted the distance that had grown between them. "Hols, we need to..."

"Who was at the door, darling? Your parents are acting even stranger than normal." Steven approached from down the hall, his view obstructed by his wife.

Breathe, Holly. She was going to hyperventilate and embarrass herself by passing out on the floor at their feet, she could see it now. Well, she could if not for the black dots dancing before her eyes. *Oh man*, he was every bit as striking as she remembered. Movie star handsome. And at one time, the love of her life. No matter how many pep-talks she'd given herself, nothing could have prepared her for this.

Her vision blurred. She leaned hard on the handle of her luggage as her knees wobbled, then gasped as the wheels slipped out from under her and she went down, landing hard on her elbow.

"Ow," she muttered, almost as an afterthought, too busy trying to control her flip-flopping tummy. "I don't feel so good." At least the tiles were cool on her back—small favors.

"Take it easy," a rich, deep voice murmured. And then he was there. Warm hands cradled her head while wide shoulders blocked the vision of Susan's surprisingly worried expression. Strange, she thought Susan would be laughing at her predicament.

"I'm fine," she snapped, wriggling to escape Steven's hold. But then she looked into his eyes and froze. Steven's eyes were the blue of a midnight sky. These eyes matched the winter storm lashing the window panes—grim and steely. "You," she whispered, stunned.

"Were you hoping for someone else?" Steven's annoying, pain-in-her-butt brother asked.

Holly lay back and closed her eyes. "Why can't I catch a break?"

ABOUT THE AUTHOR

Jacquie Biggar is a USA Today bestselling author of romance who loves to write about tough, alpha males and strong, contemporary women willing to show their men that true power comes from love. She lives on Vancouver Island with her husband and loves to hear from readers all over the world!

In her own words:

"My name is Jacquie Biggar. When I'm not acting like a total klutz, I am a wife, mother of one, grandmother, and a butler to my calico cat.

My guilty pleasures are reality tv shows like Amazing Race and The Voice. I can be found every

Monday night in my armchair plastered to the television laughing at Blake and Adam's shenanigans.

I love to hang at the beach with DH (darling hubby) taking pictures or reading romance novels (what else?).

I have a slight Tim Hortons obsession, enjoy gardening, everything pink, and talking to my friends."

facebook.com/jacqbiggar
twitter.com/jacqbiggar
instagram.com/jacqbiggar
bookbub.com/authors/jacquie-biggar
pinterest.com/jacqbiggar

ALSO BY JACQUIE BIGGAR

WOUNDED HEARTS SERIES

Tidal Falls

The Rebel's Redemption

Twilight's Encore

The Sheriff Meets His Match

Summer Lovin'

Wounded Hearts Box Set

Maggie's Revenge

With This Heart

MENDED SOULS SERIES

The Guardian

The Beast Within

Virtually Gone

GAMBLING HEARTS

Hold 'Em

Crazy Little Thing Called Love

My Girl

Married to The Texan- Box set

BLUE HAVEN

Sweetheart Cove

Sunset Beach

MEN OF WARHAWKS

Skating on Thin Ice

The Player

SINGLE TITLES

Silver Bells

The Lady Said No

My Baby Wrote Me A Letter

Tempted by Mr. Wrong

Valentine: A Hearts and Kisses Romance

Mistletoe Inn

The Sister Pact

Perfectly Imperfect

www.ingramcontent.com/pod-product-compliance
Lightning Source LLC
Chambersburg PA
CBHW061240170626
46809CB00007B/2763

* 9 7 8 1 9 8 8 1 2 6 4 0 1 *